COLLECTED STORIES

COLLECTED STORIES

OLAF STAPLEDON

ISBN: 978-93-5344-568-3

First Published: -

LECTOR HOUSE LLP
E-MAIL: lectorpublishing@gmail.com

COLLECTED STORIES

BY

OLAF STAPLEDON

CONTENTS

A MODERN MAGICIAN

THEY CONFRONTED EACH OTHER ACROSS A TEA TABLE in a cottage garden. Helen was leaning back coldly studying Jim's face. It was an oddly childish, almost foetal face, with its big brow, snub nose, and pouting lips. Childish, yes; but in the round dark eyes there was a gleam of madness. She had to admit that she was in a way drawn to this odd young man partly perhaps by his very childishness and his awkward innocent attempts at lovemaking; but partly by that sinister gleam.

Jim was leaning forward, talking hard. He had been talking for a long time, but she was no longer listening. She was deciding that though she was drawn to him she also disliked him. Why had she come out with him again? He was weedy and self-centered. Yet she had come.

Something he was saying recaptured her attention. He seemed to be annoyed that she had not been listening. He was all worked up about something. She heard him say, "I know you despise me, but you're making a big mistake. I tell you I have powers. I didn't intend to let you into my secret, yet; but, damn it, I will. I'm finding out a lot about the power of mind over matter. I can control matter at a distance, just by willing it. I'm going to be a sort of modern magician. I've even killed things by just willing it."

Helen, who was a medical student, prided herself on her shrewd materialism. She laughed contemptuously.

His face flushed with anger, and he said, "Oh very well! I'll have to show you."

On a bush a robin was singing. The young man's gaze left the girl's face and settled intently on the robin. "Watch that bird," he said. His voice was almost a whisper. Presently the bird stopped singing, and after looking miserable for a while, with its head hunched into its body, it dropped from the tree without opening its wings. It lay on the grass with its legs in the air, dead.

Jim let out a constricted squawk of triumph, staring at his victim. Then he turned his eyes on Helen. Mopping his pasty face with his handkerchief, he said, "That was a good turn. I've never tried it on a bird before, only on flies and beetles and a frog."

The girl stared at him silently, anxious not to seem startled. He set about telling her his secret. She was not bored any more.

He told her that a couple of years earlier he had begun to be interested in "all this paranormal stuff." He had been to séances and read about psychical research. He wouldn't have bothered if he hadn't suspected he had strange powers himself. He was never really interested in spooks and thought transference and so on. What fascinated him was the possibility that a mind might be able to affect matter directly. "Psychokinesis," they called this power; and they knew very little about it. But he didn't care a damn about the theoretical puzzles. All he wanted was power. He told Helen about the queer experiments that had been done in America with dice. You threw the dice time after time, and you willed them to settle with the two sixes uppermost. Generally they didn't; but when you had done a great many experiments you totted up the results and found that there had been more sixes than should have turned up by sheer chance. It certainly looked as though the mind really had some slight influence. This opened up terrific possibilities.

He began to do little experiments on his own, guided by the findings of the researchers, but also by some of his own ideas. The power was fantastically slight, so you had to test it out in situations where the tiniest influence would have detectable results, just tipping the scales.

He didn't have much success with the dice, because (as he explained) he never knew precisely what he had to do. The dice tumbled out too quickly for him. And so he only had the slight effect that the Americans had reported. So he had to think up new tricks that would give him a better opening. He had had a scientific training, so he decided to try to influence chemical reactions and simple physical processes. He did many experiments and learned a lot. He prevented a spot of water from rusting a knife. He stopped a crystal of salt from dissolving in water. He formed a minute crystal of ice in a drop of water and finally froze the whole drop by simply "willing away" all the heat, in fact by stopping all the molecular movement.

He told Helen of his first success at killing, a literally microscopic success. He brewed some very stagnant water and put a drop on a slide. Then through the microscope he watched the swarm of microorganisms milling about. Mostly they were like stumpy sausages, swimming with wavy tails. They were of many sizes. He thought of them as elephants, cows, sheep, rabbits. His idea was that he might be able to stop the chemical action in one of these little creatures and so kill it. He had read up a lot about their inner workings, and he knew what key process he could best tackle. Well, the damned things kept shifting about so fast he couldn't concentrate on anyone of them for long enough. He kept losing his victim in the crowd. However, at last one of the "rabbits" swam into a less populous part of the slide, and he fixed his attention on it long enough to do the trick. He willed the crucial chemical process to stop, and it did stop. The creature stopped moving and stayed still indefinitely. It was almost certainly dead. His success, he said, made him "feel like God."

Later he learned to kill flies and beetles by freezing their brains. Then he tried a frog, but had no success. He didn't know enough physiology to find a minute key process to check. However, he read up a lot of stuff, and at last he succeeded. He simply stopped the nerve current in certain fibres in the spinal cord that controlled the heartbeat. It was this method also that he had used on the robin.

"That's just the beginning," he said. "Soon I shall have the world at my feet.

And if you join up with me, it will be at your feet too."

Throughout this monologue the girl had listened intently, torn between revulsion and fascination. There was a kind of bad smell about it all, but one couldn't afford to be too squeamish in these days. Besides, there was probably nothing in morality, anyhow. All the same, Jim was playing with fire. Strange, though, how he seemed to have grown up while he was talking. Somehow he didn't look gawky and babyish anymore. His excitement, and her knowledge that his power was real, had made him look thrillingly sinister. But she decided to be cautious and aloof.

When at last Jim was silent, she staged a concealed yawn and said, "You're clever, aren't you! That was a good trick you did, though a horrid one. If you go much further, you'll end on the gallows."

He snorted and said, "It's not like you to be a coward."

The taunt stung her. Indignantly she answered, "Don't be ridiculous! Why should I join with you, as you call it, merely because you can kill a bird by some low trick or other?"

In Jim's life there had been certain events which he had not mentioned. They seemed to him irrelevant to the matter in hand, but they were not really so at all. He had always been a weakling. His father, a professional footballer, despised him and blamed the frail mother. The couple had lived a cat-and-dog life almost since their honeymoon. At school Jim had been thoroughly bullied; and in consequence he had conceived a deep hatred of the strong and at the same time an obsessive yearning to be strong himself. He was a bright lad and had secured a scholarship at a provincial university. As an undergraduate, he kept to himself, worked hard for a scientific degree, and aimed at a career of research in atomic physics. Already his dominant passion was physical power, so he chose its most spectacular field. But somehow his plans went awry. In spite of his reasonably good academic qualifications, he found himself stuck in a low-grade job in an industrial lab, a job which he had taken on as a stopgap till he could capture a post in one of the great institutions devoted to atomic physics. In this backwater, his naturally sour disposition became embittered. He felt he was not getting a fair chance. Inferior men were outstripping him. Fate was against him. In fact he developed something like a persecution mania. But the truth was that he was a bad cooperator. He never developed the team spirit which is so necessary in the immensely complex work of fundamental physical research. Also, he had no genuine interest in physical theory and was impatient of the necessity of advanced theoretical study. What he wanted was power, power for himself as an individual. He recognized that modern research was a cooperative affair and that in it, though one might gain dazzling prestige, one would not gain any physical power as an individual. Psychokinesis, on the other hand, might perhaps give him his heart's desire. His interest rapidly shifted to the more promising field. Henceforth his work in the lab was a mere means of earning a livelihood.

After the conversation in the cottage garden he concentrated more eagerly than ever on his venture. He must gain even more spectacular powers to impress Helen. He had decided that for him, at any rate, the promising line was to develop his skill at interfering with small physical and chemical processes, in lifeless and in living things. He learned how to prevent a struck match from lighting. He tried to bypass the whole of atomic research by applying his power of psychokinesis to the release of energy pent up in the atom. But in this exciting venture he had no success at all, perhaps because in spite of his training, he had not sufficient theoretical knowledge of physics, nor access to the right kind of apparatus for setting up the experiment. On the biological side he succeeded in killing a small dog by the same process as he had applied to the robin. He was confident that with practice he would soon be able to kill a man.

He had one alarming experience. He decided to try to stop the sparking of his motorcycle engine. He started up the bike on its stand and set about "willing" the spark to fail. He concentrated his attention on the points of the sparking plug and the leaping spark and "willed" the space between the points to become impenetrable, an insulator. This experiment, of course, involved a far greater interference with physical processes than freezing a nerve fibre or even preventing a match from lighting. Sweat poured from him as he struggled with his task. At last the engine began to misfire. But something queer happened to himself. He had a moment of horrible vertigo and nausea and then he lost consciousness. When he recovered, the engine was once more running normally.

This mishap was a challenge. He had never been seriously interested in the mere theoretical side of his experiments for its own sake, but now he had perforce; to ask himself what exactly was happening when by an "act of will" he interfered with a physical process. The obvious explanation was that in some way the physical energy that should have crossed the gap between the points had been directed into his own body; in fact that he had suffered the electric shock that he would have had if he had touched the points. It may be doubted whether the true explanation was as simple as this, for his symptoms were not those of electric shock. It might be nearer the truth to say that the inhibition of so much physical energy caused some sort of profound psychical disturbance in him; or else, to put the matter very crudely, that the physical energy was in some way converted into psychical energy in him. This theory is borne out by the fact that, when he recovered consciousness, he was in a state of great excitement and mental vigour, as though he had taken some stimulating drug.

Whatever the truth of the matter, he adopted the simpler theory and set about sidetracking the intruding energy so as to protect himself. After much anxious experimentation, he found that he could do so by concentrating his attention both on the sparking plug and on some other living organism, which then "drew off the electricity" and suffered accordingly. A sparrow sufficed. It died of the shock, while he himself remained conscious long enough to stop the engine. On another occasion he used his neighbour's dog as a "lightning conductor." The animal collapsed, but soon recovered consciousness and careened about the garden barking hilariously.

His next experiment was more exciting, and much, much more reprehensible. He went into the country and took up a position on a knoll, whence he could see a fairly long stretch of road. Presently a car came into sight. He concentrated his attention on the sparking plugs and "willed" the electrical energy to escape into the driver. The car slowed down, vacillated between the two sides of the road, and came to a standstill across the fairway. He could see the driver slumped over the steering wheel. There was no one else in the car. Greatly excited, Jim waited to see what would happen. Presently another car came in the opposite direction, hooted violently, and drew up with screeching brakes. The driver emerged, went to the derelict car, opened a door, and was confronted by the unconscious occupant. While the horrified newcomer was wondering what to do, the other recovered consciousness. There was an anxious conversation, and finally both cars went their separate ways.

Jim now felt ready to impress his girlfriend. Since the killing of the robin, they had occasionally met, and in his awkward and adolescent way he had tried to make love to her. She had always discouraged him; but she was obviously more interested in him since the robin incident. Though she sometimes affected to despise him, he felt that she was secretly drawn to him.

But one day he had an unpleasant surprise. He had boarded a bus to take him home from his work. He climbed the stairs and settled into a seat. Suddenly he noticed Helen sitting a few seats ahead with a curly-headed young man in a sportscoat. The couple were deep in conversation with their heads bent together. The girl's hair brushed his cheek. Presently she laughed, with a ring of happiness such as he had never before heard from her. She turned her face toward her companion. It was aglow with vitality and love. Or so it seemed to the jealous lover three seats behind.

Irrational fury swept over him. He was so ignorant of the ways of girls, and so indignant that "his girl" (for so he regarded her) should take notice of another man, that jealousy wholly possessed him, to the exclusion of all other considerations. He could think of nothing but destroying his rival. His gaze seized upon the nape of the hated neck before him. He passionately conjured up images of the hidden vertebrae and the enclosed bundle of nerve fibres. The nerve current must cease; must, must cease. Presently the curly head sank on Helen's shoulder, and then the whole body fell forward.

The murderer hurriedly rose from his seat and turned his back on the incipient commotion. He left the bus, as though ignorant of the disaster.

Continuing his journey on foot, he was still so excited that he had no thought but exultation over his triumph. But gradually his frenzy subsided, and he faced the fact that he was a murderer. Urgently he reminded himself that after all there was no point in feeling guilty, since morality was a mere superstition. But alas, he did feel guilty, horribly guilty; the more so since he had no fear of being caught.

As the days passed, Jim alternated between what he regarded as "irrational" guilt and intoxicating triumph. The world was indeed at his feet. But he must play his cards carefully. Unfortunately his guilt gave him no peace. He could not sleep properly; and when he did sleep, he had terrifying dreams. By day his experiments were hampered by the fantasy that he had sold his soul to the devil. This notion infuriated him with its very silliness. Yet he could not rid himself of it. He began drinking rather heavily. But he soon found that alcohol reduced his psycho-kinetic power, so he firmly broke himself of the habit.

Another possible form of relief from his obsessive guilt was sex. But somehow he could not bring himself to face Helen. He was irrationally afraid of her. Yet she must be quite ignorant that he had killed her lover.

At last he met her accidentally in the street. There was no possibility of avoiding her. She was rather wan, he thought, but she smiled at him and actually suggested a talk over a cup of coffee. He was torn between fear and desire, but presently they were seated in a cafe. After some trivial remarks, she said.

"Please comfort me! I have had a terrible shock quite recently. I was on the top of a bus with my brother who has been in Africa for three years. While we were talking, he collapsed and died almost instantly. He seemed perfectly fit. They say it was some new virus in the spinal cord." She noticed that Jim's face had turned deadly pale. "What's the matter?" she cried. "Are you going to die on me too?"

He pulled himself together and assured her that sheer sympathy for her had made him feel faint. He loved her so much. How could he help being upset by her misfortune? To his relief Helen was completely taken in by this explanation. She gave him, for the first time, the glowing smile he had formerly seen her turn upon her brother.

Encouraged, he pressed home his advantage. He said, he did so want to comfort her. They must meet again soon. And if she was at all interested in his experiments, he would show her something really exciting some time. They arranged a trip in the country the following Sunday. He privately decided to repeat for her benefit his trick with a passing car.

Sunday was a bright summer day. Sitting together in an empty railway carriage, they talked a good deal about her brother. He was rather bored, but he expressed ardent sympathy. She said she never imagined he had such a warm heart. He took her arm. Their faces drew close together, and they looked into each other's eyes. She felt an overwhelming tenderness for this strange, rather grotesque though boyish face, wherein, she told herself, the innocence of childhood was blended with an adult consciousness of power. She felt the underlying grimness, and she welcomed it. Jim, for his part, was realizing that she was very desirable. The warm glow of health had returned to her face. (Or was it a glow of love?) The full, sweet lips, the kindly, observant grey eyes, filled him not only with physical desire but a swooning gentleness that was new to him. The recollection of his guilt and present deception tormented him. An expression of misery came over his face. He let go her arm and bowed forward with his head in his hands. Perplexed and compassionate, she put an arm round his shoulders, and kissed his hair. Suddenly he burst into tears and buried his head on her breast. She hugged him and crooned over him as though he were her child. She begged him to tell her what was the matter, but he could only blubber, "Oh, I'm horrible! I'm not good enough for you."

Later in the day, however, he had quite recovered his spirits, and they walked arm in arm through the woods. He told her of his recent successes, culminating with the car incident. She was impressed and amused, but also morally shocked by the irresponsibility of risking a fatal accident merely to test his powers. At the same time she was obviously fascinated by the fanaticism that drove him to such lengths. He was flattered by her interest, and intoxicated by her tenderness and her physical proximity. For they were now resting on the little knoll where he intended to do his trick with the car, and he was lying with his head in her lap, gazing up at her face, where all the love that his life had missed seemed to be gathered. He realized that he was playing the part of an infant rather than a lover. But she seemed to need him to do so, and he was happy in his role. But soon sexual desire began to reassert itself and with it masculine self-respect. He conceived an uncontrollable lust to demonstrate his godlike nature by some formidable display of his powers. He became the primitive savage who must kill an enemy in the presence of the beloved.

Looking up through Helen's fluttering hair, he saw a small object moving. For a moment he took it for a gnat, then realized that it was a distant airplane approaching.

"Watch that plane," he said; and she was startled by the abruptness of his voice. She looked up, and down again at him. His face was contorted with effort. His eyes glared, his nostrils dilated. She had an impulse to fling him from her, so brutal he looked. But fascination triumphed. "Keep your eyes on the plane," he commanded. She looked up, then down, then up again. She knew she ought to break the devilish spell. (There was something called morality, but a delusion, probably.) Fascination had triumphed.

Presently the advancing plane's four engines hesitated, and ceased one by one to fire. The plane glided for a while, but soon gave evidence of being out of control. It vacillated, staggered, and then was in a nose dive, spiralling. Helen screamed, but did nothing. The plane disappeared behind a distant wood. After a few seconds there was a muffled crash, and smoke began to rise from behind the wood, a leaning black plume.

Jim raised himself from Helen's lap, and turning, pressed her backward to the ground. "That's how I love you," he whispered fiercely. Then he furiously kissed her lips, her neck.

She made a violent effort to pull herself together and resist the impulse of self-abandonment to this lunatic. She struggled to free herself from his grip; and presently the two stood facing each other, panting. "You're mad," she cried. "Think what you have done! You have killed people just to show how clever you are. And then you make love to me." She covered her face with her hands and sobbed.

He was still in a state of crazy exaltation, and he laughed. Then he taunted her. "Call yourself a realist! You're squeamish. Well, now you know what I am really like; and what I can do. And see! You're mine. I can kill you at any moment, wherever you are. I shall do whatever I like with you. And if you try to stop me, you'll go the way of the robin and--the man on the bus." Her hands dropped from her tear-stained face. She stared at him in mingled horror--and tenderness. She said quietly, "You're quite mad, you poor boy. And you seemed so gentle. Oh, my dear, what can I do about you?"

There was a long silence. Then suddenly Jim collapsed on the ground, blubbering like a child. She stood over him in perplexity.

While she was wondering what to do, and blaming herself for not breaking the spell before it was too late, he was in an agony of self-loathing. Then he started to use his technique upon himself, so that no more harm should be done. It was more difficult than he expected; for as soon as he began to lose consciousness he also lost his grip on the operation. But he made a desperate effort of will. When Helen, noticing his stillness, knelt down by him, he was dead.

EAST IS WEST

I LEFT MY LODGINGS IN WEST KIRBY IN THE MIDDLE OF the morning and walked along the Estuary shore, I arriving at my favourite bathing place when the tide was only a few yards from the foot of the clay cliffs. The sand, as usual on a fine Sunday, was crowded with parties, bathing and sun-bathing. I undressed and swam out till the coast was but a strip between sea and sky. At my farthest point I floated for a long while, the sun pouring through my closed eyelids. I began to feel giddy and slightly sick, so I hurried back to land.

During the rather lengthy swim I was surprised to see that the shore and the cliff-top, which I thought had been crowded, were in fact deserted. The one heap of clothes which I could detect, and which I therefore took to be my own, perplexed me by its colour. I was still more perplexed when I walked out of the water to it and found that apparently someone had removed my own flannels and had substituted a queer fancy dress of "Chinesy," pyjama-like trousers and jacket, both made of richly ornamented blue brocade. Even the towel was decorated with a Chinese or Japanese pattern; but in one corner it was marked with my own name. After a vain search for my proper clothes, I dried myself, and began experimenting with the fancy dress, shivering, and cursing the practical joker.

A bright silver coin, about the size of a florin, fell out of one of the pockets. Picking it up, I was surprised by its odd look. Closer inspection surprised me still more, for it bore on one side a grim but not unhandsome female profile, surrounded by the legend, "Godiva Dei Gra. Brit. et Gall. Reg." On the obverse was a seemingly archaic version of the royal arms, which included the French lilies but omitted the Irish harp. Round the edge I read "One Florin 1934." There were also some Japanese characters, which, to my amazement, I read. They signified, "Kingdom of Britain. Two Shillings." Other coins in the pockets proved to be of the same fantastic type. There was also a letter, in its torn envelope, inscribed in Japanese characters. I recognized the name at once as the Japanese transcription of my own. The address was that of a well-known shipping firm in Liverpool. Well-known? Collecting my wits, I realized that, familiar as it seemed, I really knew nothing about it.

By this time I was thoroughly alarmed about the state of my mind. How came it that I could read Japanese? Whence these clothes? What had become of the holiday crowd?

Since the letter was addressed to me, I read it. The writer accepted an invitation to visit me for a few days with his wife. After referring to various shipping matters, which came to me with a distressing blend of familiarity and novelty, he signed himself, if I remember rightly, "Azuki Kawamura."

Sick with cold and fright, I put on the clothes, and could not help noting that every movement executed itself with the ease of well-established habit, not with the clumsiness of one struggling with fancy dress.

I hurried along the shore toward West Kirby. With a fresh shock I discovered that the distant buildings looked all wrong. It was comforting to see that Hilbre Island at least was more or less as it should be, and that the contours of the Welsh hills across the Estuary left nothing to be desired. The black-headed gulls were indistinguishable from those of my normal experience. Half a dozen shell-duck, floating on the receding tide, were correctly attired.

Two figures approached me. What would they think of my fancy dress? But apparently it was not fancy dress; it was the orthodox costume of a gentleman. As the couple advanced, it revealed itself as a man and a girl, walking arm in arm. A few paces from me, they unlinked. He touched his cap, she curtsied. Indifferently, almost contemptuously, I acknowledged their salute. We passed.

I had been surprised to see that their dress was neither that of modern Europe nor yet Eastern like my own. It suggested a very inaccurate and ragged version of the costume of Elizabethan England as worn by the humbler sort. But he smoked a cigarette, and she bore aloft a faded Japanese sunshade.

Arriving at the town, I found that it was not West Kirby at all, not the West Kirby that I knew. The natural setting of the place was normal, but man's works were completely unrecognisable. With perfect assurance I walked along the entirely unfamiliar marine parade. The houses were mostly half-timbered, some were even thatched. But others showed unmistakably the influence of Japanese or Chinese culture. There was a "pagoda-ish" look about them. One or two were tall ferro-concrete buildings, whose vast window-space made them appear like crystal palaces. Even these betrayed in their decoration an Asiatic inspiration. It was almost as though China or Japan had been the effective centre of "Americanisation."

The parade was thronged with people of all ages and both sexes, dressed mostly in semi-Asiatic style. In some cases a native English costume had been overlaid with foreign additions, here a Chinese dragoned scarf, there a coloured sunshade. The best dressed women wore what I should describe as silk kimonos; but many of these garments were sleeveless, and none reached to the ankles. They displayed silk stockings of a type that in my own world would be regarded as European and modern, save for their great diversity and brilliance of colouring, One or two of the women, seemingly the bolder, wore very gay silk trousers and sleeveless vests. The loose brocade suits of the men were mostly of more sombre colour. I was surprised to note that many even of the best dressed promenaders had pock-marked faces. I was surprised, too, at the large number of smartly uniformed men, evidently army officers, in Robin Hood green with wide-brimmed hats. On their hips large-hilted cutlasses and neat pistol holsters combined the medieval and the modern.

The language of all these strange people was recognisably English, but of a grotesque and, I judged, a somewhat archaic type. Words of Japanese origin occurred, but not frequently. Most technical words, it seemed, were English translations of Japanese or Chinese originals. On a minute concrete building, which turned out to be a telephone call box, I noticed the phrase "Public Lightning Speaker," and under it in Japanese characters the Japanese word "Denwa."

Motors there were in plenty; but horse-drawn vehicles also, and a number of sedan chairs. Out at sea I saw a small, high-pooped, antique sailing vessel, and on the horizon a great ocean liner, trailing her black smoke.

At a certain point I turned off the Parade and passed along the shop-lined streets. The windows were all veiled for the Sabbath. Many of the large shops displayed Chinese or Japanese signs as well as English ones. I passed a small Asiatic building which I took to be a Buddhist temple. Examining the printed notices displayed at its entrance, I judged that it catered not only for Asiatic visitors but for English converts. My course now led me into the poorer quarter, and I was shocked to note the overcrowding and filth of this part of the town. Swarms of ragged urchins in native English dress played in every gutter. They had an unpleasant tendency to flee as I approached, though a few stood their ground and sullenly touched their forelocks. Many were also rickety, or covered with festering sores. In the heart of this poor district I came upon an old Gothic church. It turned out to be the parish church, and Roman Catholic. A constant stream of the devout, mostly rather shabby, flowed in at one door and out at another.

After a while the streets began to improve, and presently I emerged upon a great avenue bordered by gardens and opulent-looking houses of the sort which I now recognized as both Asiatic and modern.

One of these pocket-mansions was apparently my own, for I entered it without permission. It was a delightful, even a luxurious building, and I reflected that changing my world I had also "gone up in the world."

At the sound of my entry a manservant appeared in a vaguely "Beefeater" kind of livery. Flinging him my bathers and towel, I opened a door out of the entrance hall and went into a sitting room. Before I had time to study it, a woman rose from some cushions on the floor and caught me in her arms.

"Tom! Base Tom," she said, smiling gaily. "'Tis but a month since we wed, and already thou art entarded for thy Sunday dinner! Foolish me to let thee practice thy Asiatic water-vice unkeepered!"

A bachelor, I might have shown some confusion at this reception, but I found myself embracing her with proprietary confidence and zestfully kissing her lips.

"Sweet Betty, let me envisage thee," I said, "to see if thou art worn with pining for me."

So this was my wife, and her name was Betty, and we had been married a month and were evidently still very pleased about it. She was fair, superbly Nordic. Behind the sparkle of her laughing eyes I detected a formidable earnestness. She was tall. Her green silk kimono veiled the contours of an Amazon. As she broke from me and swept through the door, smiling over her shoulder, I wondered how I had ever persuaded such a splendid creature to marry me.

The gong (a Chinese bronze) was sounding for our Sunday dinner. I rushed upstairs to wash, but on the landing I encountered our Japanese guests. He was a slim middle-aged figure in brocade of decent grey. She, much younger, was slight, trousered in deep blue shantung, and vested in crimson. The light was behind her, and I saw almost nothing of her face.

I bowed deeply and began to speak in Japanese. It was rather terrifying to watch the appropriate thoughts emerge in my mind and embody themselves fluently in a language of which I supposed myself to be completely ignorant. "I hope, sir, that you had a successful morning, and that you will not have to leave us again today. We should like to take you to call on some friends who long to meet you." The couple returned my salute, I thought, rather sadly. I was soon to discover that they had reason for gloom.

"Alas," he said, "our experience this morning suggests that we had better not appear in public more than we can help. Since the crisis, your countrymen do not like the Yellows. If you still permit, we will stay with you till my business is done and our ship sails; but for your sakes and our own, it is better that we should not risk further trouble." I was about to protest, but he raised his hand, smiled, and ushered his wife downstairs.

After washing in the tiled and chromium-plated bathroom (the taps screwed the wrong way), I hurried into our bedroom to brush my hair. It was a relief to find that the mirror still showed my familiar face; but whether through the refreshment of the bathe or owing to more enduring causes, I appeared rather healthier and more prosperous than was customary in my other world.

On the dressing table was a newspaper. The bulk of it was written in English, but a few columns and a few advertisements were in Japanese. I vaguely remembered reading it in bed over an early cup of tea. It was called, I think, The Sunday Watchman. I opened it, and discovered on the main page, in huge headlines, "Ultimatum to the Yellow Peoples. Hands off Europe. Britain will defend her allies."

Betty's clear voice bade me hurry, and not be so "special" over my toilet.

When I arrived downstairs, she was explaining to the guests, in her serviceable but rather inaccurate Japanese, that she had again taken them at their word, and ordered a typical English meal for them. "Although," she said, with the faintest emphasis, "we ourselves are now more used to Eastern diet."

It fell to me to carve the roast beef of old England and at the same time to make conversation in Japanese. To judge by the ease with which I combined these actions, both must have been familiar.

Yet every moment of my experience was completely novel and fantastic. With curiosity and yet familiarity my eyes roamed about the room. The dinner service was of China, in both senses. To be in keeping with the affectedly native meal it should have been of pewter or wood. With some amusement I noted our elegant little thin-stemmed, flat-bowled sake cups, of silver, gold-inlaid. These I had bought in Nagasaki on my last visit to the East. Evidently my wife had been unable to resist the temptation of displaying them, though they were quite incongruous in a sample English meal. The furniture was vaguely Tudor, so to speak. On the walls hung painted silks which I knew to be Chinese and Japanese, though some of them were confusingly reminiscent of modernist European art in my other world. I regarded with special pride and affection a tall silken panel on which was very delicately and abstractly suggested a slender waterfall surrounded by autumnal trees. Wreaths of mist or spray veiled the further foliage. Above, and more remote, domes of forest, receding, one behind the other, loomed ghostly through clouds. "Forest on forest hung about his head," I murmured to myself, and wondered whether in my new, strange world Keats had any footing. This much prized panel, this silken forest of copper and gold and pearl grey, I had bought from an artist in Tokyo.

The company was as hybrid as the room. Two English maidservants in mob-caps and laced bodices moved demurely in the background. Opposite me sat my exquisitely English wife, the warm tone of her sunned arms contrasting with the cool parchment-like skin of the Japanese lady. The grave and slightly grizzled Mr. Kawamura was typical (I half guessed it, half remembered) of the finer sort of Japanese man of affairs. He was a "shipping director," which was the Japanese equivalent of a ship owner. That is, he was a civil servant in control of a line of steamers. In Japan, I recollected, all the means of production were now state-owned.

This fact, along with others that cropped up in the course of conversation, made me revise my view of the relation of my new world to my old. I had guessed that the roles of Japan and Britain were simply reversed. But evidently the situation was more complicated that that, for Japan was some sort of socialist state. I was soon to have further evidence of complication.

My intense curiosity about everything, and my anxiety lest my own behaviour should betray me, bid fair to be eclipsed by a third interest, namely the fascination of Mrs. Kawamura's personality. I was at first inclined to think of her as a modernized and world-conscious reincarnation of the Lady Murasaki; but presently I learned that she was in fact a native not of Japan but of China. Though her shining black hair was cut short, and her whole bearing, like her dress, was frankly modern, her features (of old ivory) and also her grave intelligent expression suggested the ancient culture of her race. In spite of her "shingle" and bare arms, she reminded me of a certain very delicate Chinese miniature painter and embroidered on silk. This I had long ago encountered in my other world, and its pale perfect face had become my symbol of all the best in China. Mrs. Kawamura's was this face done large and with an added largeness of spirit. Her heavy eyelids gave her an expression of perpetual meditation. A sweet and subtle mockery played about her eyes and lips. But more particularly I was intrigued by her manner, by the way in which she moved her hands and turned her head. Her whole demeanour reminded me of the action of an artist engaged on some very precise but ample piece of brush-work, so exact it was, yet flowing.

Between the courses Mrs. Kawamura drew a cigarette case from her pochette and asked if it was permitted to smoke at such an early stage in an English meal. Betty, after a minute pause, hastened to say, "Why, of course, in the houses of those who have travelled." Up to this point I had played my part without a single lapse, but now at last I tripped. Automatically I produced a matchbox from my pocket, struck a light, and offered it for her convenience. Mrs. Kawamura hesitated for a moment, looked me in the eyes, glanced at my wife, then smilingly shook her head and used her own cigarette lighter. Betty, I saw, was blushing and trying not to show bewilderment and distress. In a flash it came upon me that in England (of this new world) one did not offer to light a woman's cigarette unless one was very intimate with her. I began to stammer an apology; but Mr. Kawamura saved the situation with a laugh, and said to Betty, "Your husband forgot that he is no longer in Japan, where that action is considered only common politeness." I snatched at this excuse. "Yes," I said, "I grew so used to it. And today I have had too much sun." It was Betty's turn to laugh, as best she could. Lapsing into English, she said, "Thy Oriental ways keep surprising me, Tom, but I expect I shall get used to them." In Japanese she added, "Of course England is rather stupid about some things."

Mrs. Kawamura leaned toward Betty and lightly touched the hand that still nervously crumbled a piece of bread. There was nothing of patronage in the act; or if there was, it was rendered inoffensive by the sincere and rather timid respect of the culture which is already in full and determinate blossom for the culture which has still to unfold. "You English women," she said, "have a great task. You have to see that your men preserve what is best in England while they absorb what is best in the East." Smiling at her husband, she continued, "Men are all such boys. They run after flashy new things and throwaway the well-tried old things. Azuki, there, is much more interested in his new turbo-electric liner than in the incomparable literature of my country." This mischievous sally was evidently well directed, for Mr. Kawamura responded with amiable indignation, asserting his claim to be an amateur of letters, and adding that if no one thought about ships and other practical matters, no one would have leisure to enjoy Chinese literature.

Thus far the talk had avoided the subject which was in all our minds, the international crisis. By common consent we had spoken only of personal matters, of a Kawamura nephew who was studying in Canton and of Betty's young sister, at an Orientalised school in London. But the conversation was now definitely turned to the differences between East and West. Our guests generously praised the courage and enterprise which, within eighty years, had changed Britain from a feudal to a modern industrial community of the first rank. To this I politely replied that we had but copied what Japan's genius had created. For had not the Japanese been the pioneers of mechanical invention and commercial organization during four of the most momentous centuries of human history? "If at the dawn of our era, after Rome's fall, we English had been as great seamen as the Japanese have always been, we might have forestalled you. But though Nordic sea-rovers contributed to our racial stock, we did not preserve their maritime habits. Nor did the continent of Europe." The words slid easily from my lips, but they were startling news to my mind.

Mrs. Kawamura remarked that in the East there was now a strong conviction that commercialism and mechanization had in fact done more harm than good. It had blinded the great majority to all that was most desirable in life. Were not the

English now in grave danger of ruining their own admirable native culture in their haste to dominate the world with their new industrial power? "To us," she said, "it seems terrible that, in spite of our tragic example, you should plunge blindly into the modern barbarism and grossness from which we ourselves are only today struggling to escape. And now, just when we are at last finding the beginnings of peace and wisdom and general happiness, when the Chinese nations are at last outgrowing their age-old enmities, when all the Yellow Peoples are becoming reconciled even to the half-European but mellowing culture of Russia, must we be drawn into this terrible quarrel between yourselves and New Nippon? If there is war, how can I ever think of you two dear English people as my enemies?"

At the mention of New Nippon, I remembered with a shock of surprise the great independent Federation which included the whole of North America. This vast community was formerly the most successful of Japan's colonies and had since become the mightiest of all the "Eastern Powers."

"But why," I asked, "should you come in at all? This quarrel is so remote from you. You have no longer any European possessions except Gibraltar, which you are in the very act of selling to us. Your empire has fallen from you, and you are happier without it. Your reduced population makes you far less dependent on foreign trade than formerly. Your traditional championship of the oppressed should induce you to side with us, or at least not against us. And what have you to gain by coming in? Your social conditions are the envy of the East, and of the West also. And though you are politically eclipsed, you share with North China the cultural leadership of the world. War will simply destroy all this. If you come in, you will merely be used as a tool by your more powerful and less civilized kinsmen. But why should there be any question of your coming in?"

"Why indeed?" said Mr. Kawamura. Then, after a pause, "The true reason, I think, is this. Though we have lost our empire we are still bound to it. Our former dominions in South Africa and South Nippon" (by this name I knew he referred to Australia) "and our ally the Maori Kingdom, have a firm hold on us. Such foreign trade as we have (and we do still need foreign trade) is nearly all of it trade with them. Well, some of those former dominions are terribly frightened of your rising power. They have large unoccupied territories; while you and your inseparable allies the Irish are over-crowded. We have long ago learned to control the growth of our population, but you persist in refusing to do so. Inevitably then you must expand. Together with Ireland, and with the support of your European dependencies, you constitute a formidable military power." Here he hesitated. "Your imperialism is at least as ruthless as ours was in the old days. Our former colonies know well that you will attack them sooner or later. Better at once, they say, before you are invincible."

Betty broke in to say, "But surely you see that we must free Europe. I know our policy has often been harsh and provoking. I am not one of those who think we are always right. But this time we must be firm. It's a solemn duty."

"Well," continued Mr. Kawamura, "on the whole you have a pretty strong case; though of course we can't believe you are really going to free Europe. You are going to take over the management of Europe from New Nippon. That is the real aim of your elder statesmen. Anyhow, I personally agree that it is folly for Japan to come into the war. But racial passion has been roused, partly by the propaganda of trade interests in New Nippon, partly by your own press. And your Queen, your great but dangerous Queen, has said things which were bound to enrage the less balanced sections of our public."

"Yes, Azuki," said Mrs. Kawamura. "But surely by now the less balanced sections of our public have very little effect on government action. After all, since our Great Change we are rapidly becoming civilized enough and cosmopolitan enough to laugh at a few cattish insults." She checked herself, smiled deprecatingly at Betty, and proceeded. "No, if our government wanted to keep out, it could. But somehow it seems to lack the courage to do so. I wonder whether New Nippon has some horrible secret financial control over us. Not that we can actually help them much by coming in. But the wealthy caste of New Nippon are inclined to hate us because we have learned the lesson that they cannot bring themselves to learn. They know that war would ruin our modest prosperity and make nonsense of our new, hard-won culture. Might they not bring us in for sheer spite?"

Her husband raised his eyebrows, and said nothing. The dessert was now over, and we moved into our "withdrawing room." Here there was rather more of Japanese influence than in the dining room. The furniture was of lacquer. A great stone or concrete fireplace, however, betrayed the English character of the house.

Tea was served in cups of eggshell china, which Mrs. Kawamura tactfully admired. Betty explained with some self-consciousness that though tea was not included in the orthodox English diet, we had grown very dependent on this most refreshing Oriental drink and could not face the prospect, of doing without it after our Sunday dinner. The habit was indeed rapidly spreading.

Before seating myself I had picked up a large book which I rightly expected to be an atlas. During the ensuing conversation I turned over its pages. I came first on a map of the British Isles. The "Kingdom of Ireland" was coloured green, the Kingdoms of England and Scotland red. Towns, mountains, and rivers mostly bore familiar names. A population map revealed the well-known concentrations around London and in the industrial North, but towns and rural areas were both more populous than in my "other world." Ireland, moreover, contained almost as many people as England, presumably because throughout its history it had developed as an independent community. The total population of the British Isles was over seventy million.

Turning to a map of Europe, I found the northern half of France labelled "Kingdom of France," and coloured red, like Britain. The Netherlands and all the coastlands of the Western Baltic appeared pink and were dubbed "Liberated Nordic Principalities." Pink proved to be the colour of "British Protectorates and Dependencies." Most of these principalities, together with much of Central Europe and Italy, were embraced within a crimson border. Across this vast territory was printed "Holy Roman Empire." This region, and indeed most of Europe, was divided into a mosaic of principalities, duchies, free cities. Scattered around all the coasts of the continent were little patches of yellow, the largest of which included Hamburg. The key gave yellow as "Terrains seized by New Nippon." Large tracts in the Iberian Peninsula, the Balkans, Western Russia, and the eastern marches of the Empire were coloured buff and labelled "War Lords," or "No Settled Government," or "Workers' Councils." The eastern half of Russia bore the legend, "Union of Socialist Conciliar Republics."

A map of the world showed this "Soviet" Union (if I may so translate it) as extending to the Pacific. Its centre of gravity was evidently well to the east, for its capital was a town not far from the Chinese frontier, bearing a Mongolian name unfamiliar to me. China consisted of three great republics. Korea and Manchuria were independent "Empires." India was a congeries of native states. Across the whole subcontinent was printed, "Aryan Peoples Liberated from Japan," with appropriate dates. Many others were coloured with the yellow of; New Nippon. That most formidable of the "Eastern" Powers, which extended from the Arctic to Mexico, was covered with Japanese names. Its capital was a city where San Francisco should have been. In South America, which was cut up into many states, such names as were not native were obviously of Chinese origin. In place of the three great British dominions of the Southern Hemisphere appeared "Nippon in Afric," "South Nippon," and "Maori Kingdom," all of them independent.

While I was still poring over the atlas, the church clock chimed the hour. Betty rose, saying to the guests, "It is almost time for the Queen's speech. I hope you will excuse us if we listen, for it is a solemn duty for all Britons to hear Her Majesty today." The Kawamuras assured her that, though they could not understand English, they would gladly listen to the world-famous voice. Betty thanked them, pressed the switch, and resumed her seat.

The news bulletin was being announced in an intensively cultivated English voice. The language was a kind of English which in my "other world" I should have regarded as a fantastic hybrid of Babu and Elizabethan. Familiar words bore strange yet intelligible meanings, or were piquantly misshapen. As I listened I interjected an occasional sentence of Japanese translation for our guests. If my memory is faithful, what I heard was roughly as follows; but much of the linguistic oddity has escaped me.

In the East End of London, the voice assured us, revulsion was now stilled. The Lord High Sheriff, mindful of the foreign peril, had gripped this homely peril firmly. He was resolved to convince the erring commonalty of that region that they had been abduced by foreign tongue-wielders, and that the witful British people would none of their treason. All good Europeans should be mindful that, though Russia was partly European, the dangerous political thoughts of the Conciliar Union and its emissaries were wholly Asiatic. The Lord Sheriff had therefore encompassed the whole revulsive region in a martial cincture. Two warships in the Thames had cast shell on Poplar and Canning Town, till all the rebel holds were disrupted. Soon after dawn the obsedient troops advanced. Their compressive movement met no repugnance. The rebels abjected their arms, and twelve score ringleaders were enchained. These were judged; and duly hanged, drawn, and quartered, in the presence of a God-thanking crowd. Some thousands of the less outstanding rebels were being concentered in temporary castrations, afield in Essex, to await Her Majesty's pleasure.

After a pause the voice resumed in an awed tone which skillfully suggested suppressed excitement. Listeners, it said, were now to hear the living voice of their Sovereign. When the speaker solemnly commanded all who heard to stand, Betty and I promptly rose to our feet. Our guests, after one bewildered glance, followed suit. In an awed monotone, the announcer proclaimed: "Her Most Pure and Invincible Majesty, Godiva, by the Grace of God, Defender of the Christian Faith, Protector of the Holy Roman Empire, Queen."

After another pause another voice possessed the air, a somewhat husky, but regal, and withal seductive contralto.

"My subjects! My most loyal friends, English and Scottish! And ye, my few but faithful Welsh! All, all whose home is Britain, this demi-paradise, as our immortal Strongbow names it, this insel set in the silver sea. And you, my gallant French! And all my indefatigable Teutons! Others, too, I call; you my loving neighbors in the Green Isle, subjects of my dear cousin Shean. And not only to these I speak, but to all Europeans, of whatever nation and estate. For all, all of us together, are now affronted by this most severe and instant peril. Oh my peoples, all mine in spirit, though not all in title! Our homely differings now slip from us. We remind us only that we are one kin, colleagued together at last against the cunning, the heartless, the lascivious and Godless Yellows.".

Such undiplomatic language was startling, even from our outspoken Queen. Explanation was soon to follow.

"It is not long since the last great war obtended its dark bloody wings over our continent. I myself, though scarce in the full bloom of my womanhood," (Betty at this point made a movement of surprise) "even I can remember the victorious geste of British and French hosts against the heroic but miswitting Germans, whom foreign devils had abduced. I can recall well the day, soon after the handfasting of the peace, when I, the child Queen of Britain, was plauded by the rejoyed Parisians and crowned Queen of France, thereby resuming the lapsed title of my forebears. I can remember how the North German lords, who had by then destrued their own traitorous princes, now wishfully and gladly laid their crownlets at my feet, my small ensatined feet."

Here the Queen paused. Mrs. Kawamura took the opportunity of disposing of a lengthy and precarious cigarette ash. Our eyes met. She knew no English, but it seemed that merely through the Queen's vocal demeanour she sensed the essence of the situation. I shall not forget how, when I had signalled mock distress, the noncommittal politeness of her glance was lit by relief and sad amusement.

Her Majesty continued. "Oh, Great White Peoples, since that war, much has happened. Through all those years I have striven to be worthy of the task which the ensworded Christ has set upon me, the delivery of Europe. For let us remind ourselves of well-known truth. In all our churches, our divine and most courageous Captain hangs crossed upon the blade and hilt of the Sword. That same Sword, when he had risen from the dead, he himself grasped, and wields today, leading the Faithful. He came not to bring peace. And I, though till today I have besieged my just aims by parley, am his lieutenant. Though it was by parley and fine machinations that I and my counsellors defted the Japanese from all their treaty ports, it was the springing strength of my army and navy and my aerials that rendered those pacific arguments convictive. But now, today, argument has failed; and I am here to call upon you, all White Peoples, to take arms in earnest. For the hour has come when we must constrain New Nippon to disgorge her rapine, or else betray irrevocably the cause for which we stand together."

Strange, I thought to myself, that only yesterday, before I had my mysterious dream of the other world (for I was beginning to reverse my view as to which world was real and which was fantasy) I might have applauded the Queen's apologia! And there stood Betty, till now my soul's twin, drinking the royal words with no misgiving.

The Queen continued. "I have recently and justly claimed on behalf of the Germans, Hamburg; for the French, Bordeaux; and for the Lambards, Genova. As ye already wit, Europeans, parley having failed, I have been constrained, after close heart-prying, to obdict an ultimatum. But what I shall now tell you, my peoples, will be newspell to you. Prevising clearly the rebutment of that ultimatum, I forestalled the New Nippon retort. I struck. And already, even as I speak they bring me word that Hamburg's defences have been destrued by my brave aerials. A gallant geste, and most enheartening newspell, oh White Peoples! But let us not deceive ourselves. Dire days leap toward us. The whole force of New Nippon and of the Chinese Republic, and haply of Japan also, will be oppugned against us. Nothing can save us now but crazy hardihood."

Again the Queen paused. Betty's large eyes sought mine, but I dared not face them. Mrs. Kawamura's had found diversion in watching a tomtit through the window. Her husband was obviously wondering if he could sit without committing lese majeste.

The royal voice resumed. "Oh men and women of Europe! We shall one and all be stricken by the hugest and most contorturous of wars. The sky will rain fire and poison. Millions shall die. But oh Europeans, let such as die, die singing to the ensworded Christ, whose truth we stand for. Let such as live, live hate fast toward the Yellows, till all the coasts of Europe be purged of these slot-eyed commercers of the East: who suck and squander the natural wealth of our continent; who undo the native toughness of our bodies by teaching us their own soft life; who undo the strength of our souls by logiking that our holy Church is founded on lies, and that our Christ, like their own Buddha, prized gentleness above fortitude. They gave us opium. They have tempted our coupling lovers with filthy lore to prevent the sacred burden of motherhood, hoping thereby to thin our numbers. Women of Europe, consider! In Japan, so little do men prize virtue, that husbands lend out their wives to any guest for the night. And what wives, what women! Painted! Lewdly exhibiting their jaundy breasts, and..."

I sprang to the radio and snapped the switch. "Tom, Tom," cried Betty, gripping my arm. "What ails thee? Her Majesty! If someone should have heard you check her!" Then laughter seized me. Mrs. Kawamura smiled, perplexed, demure. Mists and irrelevant shapes came before my eyes. Still laughing, I woke in my "other world." I was in the horsehair chair by the fireplace in my lodging-house sitting room. My landlady, who was clearing away my Sunday dinner, was laughing too, apparently at something I had said or done, for she now remarked, "Well, you are a queer one!" The lace curtains fluttered by the open window. In the garden my "bather" and towel were swinging on the clothesline.

ARMS OUT OF HAND

SIR JAMES TOOK UP HIS PEN FOR THE FATEFUL LETTER. He wrote the date and "Dear Councillor Saunderson." Then his hand stayed motionless. The words that should have followed were ready in his mind, but his hand refused to move. The fingers slackened. The pen slipped from his grip, and rolled away. He tried to pick it up, but his right arm was impotent.

Startled and alarmed, he nevertheless felt, and quickly suppressed, a flash of glee; the letter would have to be postponed. He rose from his desk. His arm fell loose at his side, and dangled like the neck of a freshly killed fowl. Anxiously, he tried his other limbs, and found them normal. But he could no more move his right arm than shift a mountain. He crossed the room, and collapsed in an easy chair. The paralysed arm swung behind him, so that he sat heavily on the hand. No pain, no sensation at all, was felt in the sick member.

Sir James Power was a successful and respected citizen. He had climbed to his present position by sheer hard work and intelligence. Managing director and principal shareholder of a large store in a large provincial city, he prided himself equally on the efficiency of his business and his treatment of his employees. Good conditions, good wages, a profit-sharing scheme, and generous care in sickness afforded them all that they could reasonably demand. True, he expected them to work, and to keep his regulations; and also to show the same devotion to the firm as he himself had always shown. He was never tired of telling them that they were public servants, not merely servants of a private firm. Somehow his exhortations did not have the effect that he wished. A few of the staff did indeed respond with devotion, but less through loyalty to the firm and its social function than through personal respect for himself. But others, in fact the great majority, seemed to be quite cynically concerned with their own interests, believing apparently that he was no more public-spirited than they were themselves. His exhortations they regarded as mere tricks of the slave-driver bent on private profit. Very few (he felt) had the imagination to realize that the motive of all his own hard work was sheer public service. Still less did they understand that he cared for their welfare as though they were his children.

It was because of his public position that he felt bound to write the letter. He must protest against the treatment of certain hot-headed young men by the police; and his first step must be a private protest to the member of the City Council who, according to his information, had instigated police action. The young men were unemployed and had brought themselves into bad odour with the authorities by organizing demonstrations of the unemployed. They had succeeded in arousing considerable public hostility to the great steel firm that had formerly employed them. Councillor Saunderson was the head of that firm. The leaders of the protest movement had been very careful to keep within the law. The police for long failed to find a sound reason for interfering. But at last they raided the head-quarters of the movement and found a large number of leaflets, which, with a stretch of the imagination, could be interpreted as seditious and moreover as aimed at the troops. The details of the case do not concern this account of Sir James' strange illness. Suffice it that the young men were at last jailed, and that Sir James, as a staunch defender of the rights of the individual, had been urgently appealed to by several worthy societies to use his influence on their behalf. He had been very reluctant to take action. He had always insisted that his interest in politics was confined to the defence of individual freedom and private enterprise. Hence his choice of a political party. But the violent ideas of Communism were obviously causing unrest among the discontented sections of society, and they would have to be suppressed before matters became serious. He knew almost nothing about Communism as a political theory, and cared less. But one thing he reckoned he did know. In this critical period, revolutionary ideas were dangerous. Moreover, his own experience of men had taught him that private enterprise in pursuit of one's own interest was the lifeblood of society. And as to unemployment, it was unfortunately necessary to put up with a good deal of it in times of depression so that there might be a sufficient labour pool in times of prosperity.

It was for these reasons that Sir James was so painfully torn over the writing of the letter. His habitual loyalty to the idea of freedom compelled him to write it; but as a believer in law and order and a supporter of the existing social system, he was on the side of authority against irresponsible agitators. Moreover, in writing the letter he must inevitably come into conflict with eminent citizens and mighty forces. He fully realized that to write the letter was to range himself on the side of riffraff and against highly respected persons with whom he had always managed to keep on good terms. His action would be treated as a declaration of war. Moreover, the public enquiry which he must demand might reveal certain facts in his own career, facts which, though not illegal, would somehow look a little incongruous in the life of an exceptionally upright man and a champion of liberty. Indeed his enemies would be able to put quite a sinister interpretation on them.

For Sir James himself had sometimes been ruthless with his employees. He had acted on the principle that, to prevent the perversion of the many, one must sometimes crush the few, even if by methods not publicly sanctioned. A few years earlier, certain members of his staff had begun to spread Communist doctrines among their colleagues. They had succeeded in rousing a certain amount of discontent, and might in time undermine the morale of the whole staff. In deciding to interfere, Sir James was of course not concerned with politics but simply with the efficiency of his business. It had been a ticklish matter. He was particularly anxious to avoid the charge that he had dismissed the agitators because of their political opinions. He had therefore ingeniously arranged for them to find themselves in a position of great temptation. The details, once more, are irrelevant. Suffice it that they were given the opportunity of stealing the firm's property on a large scale.

Two of them succumbed to the temptation, were caught in the act, convicted, and jailed. It had been easy to dismiss the others as suspects.

Unfortunately certain individuals who had helped to set the trap were no longer under Sir James' control. They had already tried to damage his reputation by telling the story, but hitherto no one had believed them. How could anyone be expected to believe such a charge brought against a highly respected alderman by persons who obviously bore him a grudge. Sir James' new enemies, however, would be only too glad to use the information to raise a scandal. So in more ways than one it had been hard for him to bring himself to the point of writing the letter.

And now at the last moment a strange fate had thwarted him.

For, some minutes Sir James sat in his big leather-covered chair, wondering whether he had had a stroke. Obviously he ought to call the doctor at once, but somehow he did not. He prided himself on being an exceptionally healthy man and on his power of overcoming minor ailments by methods spiritual rather than medical. He was not actually a Christian Scientist but he believed that the best cure for most diseases was a combination of prayer and a refusal to admit that one was ill. Physical illness, he secretly believed, was always a sign of spiritual illness. The fact that he himself was so healthy was probably his main reason for this belief. Medicine, he was convinced, was mainly quackery. Fresh air, exercise, temperate eating, and "total abstinence" were all that were necessary on the physical side. For the rest, if you could face God with a good conscience, He would keep you fit.

But this sudden affliction? Surely he was still far too young to begin breaking up. Though he was well on in the forties, everyone said he looked ten years younger. Of course he had been overstraining himself lately, what with his growing business and his increasingly active public life. And in the last few weeks there had been this quite exceptional worry, culminating in the need to write that letter. It was grievously tempting to shirk this duty, for he could so easily let the whole matter slide. Yes, but everyone would know that he had deliberately kept silent, and betrayed all that he had stood for in the life of the Chapel, all those lay sermons he had preached on business morality, and the trusteeship of the heads of industry and of the city fathers.

The thing must be done. Emphatically he stubbed his cigarette; and suddenly realized that he was doing it with his right hand. He moved the arm about to test it. He rose and picked up a chair. He held it out at arm's length. Apparently all was well again, and he even began to wonder whether the whole affair had been some sort of illusion.

Once more he sat down at his desk, and with a sigh he took up his pen. For a while he considered the right opening, but his mind soon wandered off in reverie. Then suddenly he came to with the startling discovery that after "My Dear Councillor Saunderson," he had written, "You treated those young swine the right way, and you can count on my support. If people like us don't take a strong line and stand together, we shall lose control. Good luck, you old bugger!"

Sir James snatched up the letter with his left hand, crumpled it, and threw it into the fire. He took another sheet and began again. "My dear," but his right arm again became paralysed. He rose and walked about the room. Presently he noticed that he was blowing his nose with his right hand. The arm was normal again.

At this point his secretary came in to consult him about a doubtful passage in some scribbled notes that he had given her to type. Miss Smith, Mildred to her family, was something more than the ideal secretary. On the telephone she had of course a voice like sunshine. Her shorthand and typing were of course perfect. She knew almost as much about the business as the Managing Director, for on many occasions he had taken her into his confidence. More remarkable, she had such a gift of intuitive insight into human character that her employer often consulted her about members of the staff; and he had learned to rely on her judgment. She had even been known to criticize Sir James himself, and he to act upon her criticism. She would generally make her point indirectly, and with such tact and humour that the implied censure could be acted on without loss of dignity. Nearly always her criticism took the form of revealing the other person's point of view more clearly than Sir James had been able to conceive it and of suggesting a line of action less high-handed than he had intended.

In spite of her remarkable virtues, she was not perfect. Sometimes her employer had to reprimand her for allowing her sense of humour to run riot. There was an occasion when, at the end of a painful interview with a junior member of the staff, he had been forced to sack the young man for insolence. Miss Smith had afterwards told Sir James that he had "looked like a cat bitten by the mouse it was playing with." He made it clear to her that he was not amused.

In addition to her other assets, Miss Smith had charm. She was not, according to conventional standards, a beauty. Her nose was a dainty but undignified little mushroom; her mouth was more humorous than seductive. But her features were adequate, and a bright and generous spirit seemed to light them up from within. This charm of hers she used very effectively in her employer's service, protecting him from unwanted callers without causing offence, and so on. She also used it on her employer himself. Who can blame a pretty woman, conscious of her charm, but also of her sincerity and efficiency, for using all her art to persuade this handsome, upright, wealthy, and distinguished knight that they two were destined for one another? She felt sure, moreover, that, in an obscure way, he was already in love with her, though he would not allow himself to notice such a disturbing fact. Of course, though he treated her always with a very special consideration and respect, he had never (he supposed) encouraged her to hope for anything more intimate. Indeed she herself wondered how she dared expect him ever to offer her more. He was so far above her; and so busy that he simply had no time to notice her, save as an efficient secretary, and just now and then as a junior friend. Yet she was convinced that he needed her, not merely as a secretary but as a mate.

The great man and his secretary stood poring over the pencilled sheets. Suddenly she exclaimed, "Oh, please, Sir James, you mustn't!" Not till that moment was he aware that his right arm had encircled her waist and that his right hand was hungrily feeling about her person. Unwittingly he had pressed her to his side with considerable vigour, and to his dismay he found that he could not release her. The limb acted on its own, and he could no more control it than one can inhibit vomiting or sneezing when these reflexes are already going forward. She gently struggled to free herself. His grip tightened. "Please, please let me go!" she implored him; but he wailed in answer, "I can't let you go, I can't." Whereupon Miss Smith, though generally so adept at sensing personal situations, for once made a grave mistake. Taking this remark as a confession of uncontrollable love, she sighed "Oh, my dear," and laid her head on his shoulder. But he protested, "It's not me, it's my arm. Something awful has happened to it." He vainly tried with his left hand to unclasp his right arm. But now she, realizing that she had made a fool of herself, pressed both hands against his chest and broke away. "My profound apologies," he gasped, panting with his right arm's exertion, "but believe me, Miss Smith, I am really ill, and I couldn't control my arm at all." She had hurried to the door. Hastily he added, "I suppose you will want to leave me. I will do all I can to help you to find a good post. Please, please, believe me that I meant no disrespect." With a hand on the doorknob she turned and looked at him. He was standing with bowed head almost like a naughty schoolboy. His right arm hung limply. For a full minute she watched him; then unlatched the door, then closed it. Presently she said, "I do indeed believe you. But oh what a fool I must seem to you!" Controlling her emotion as best she could, she added shakily, "I don't want to leave you. You'll need me, and I want to help you. But oh, I can't stay now." There was silence. Then he said, almost in a whisper, "Very humbly, very, very humbly, I ask you to stay."

The telephone rang in the outer office, and Miss Smith hurried away to answer the call. Employer and secretary were soon immersed in the business of the day. Neither made any reference to the recent trouble, and the rebel arm fulfilled its normal tasks as though nothing had happened. But the letter was not written.

Before leaving at the end of the day, Miss Smith had urged Sir James to call in a doctor, but he was not persuaded. He allowed her, however, to cancel his engagement to speak that evening at the Christian Forum. After dining alone he retired to his study for coffee and a smoke. The cat was curled up in his armchair. It was the one creature whose presence he found entirely easeful and delightful. He lifted it gently and sat down with it in his lap. Sipping his coffee, pulling at his pipe, occasionally stroking the cat's sleek black coat, he pondered on the events of the day. It seemed impossible that his arm should ever have run amok, so quietly and naturally the fingers passed over the silken fur. Purring, the cat extended itself up his waistcoat. He scratched behind its ears. Suddenly his fingers seized the animal by the neck ad gripped it savagely. It struggled and fought. In horror Sir James tried with his left hand to rescue the cat, but his right arm held the animal out at arm's length, and well to the side, so that the left arm could not reach it. He rose from his chair and tried to jamb his right arm against the wall so as to flex it and bring the hand within reach of his left hand. The muscles of his shoulders and chest were strained in a painful conflict, some obedient to the strange will that possessed the right arm, some to Sir James himself. The right arm remained stiff as a rod. The grip seemed superhumanly powerful, for the cat's tongue was forced out, and it could not make a sound. Presently its struggles weakened, then ceased. The hand released it, and it fell limply to the ground. The arm too fell limply, paralysed. Sir James knelt beside the cat in great distress, whimpering, "Oh God, what have I done!" The cat was still alive, and already showing signs of recovery. With both arms he picked it up and laid it on a cushion in front of the fire. Then he crept miserably into his easy chair feeling shattered and faint.

Obviously he must telephone to the doctor; but when he had at last forced himself to accept his fate, and had already reached out his hand for the receiver, it occurred to him that the doctor would certainly turn him over to a psychiatrist. All this mind-healing was worse than quackery; it was diabolical, and terribly dangerous. These people, he was convinced, were instruments of Satan. They made a fetish of sex, and their whole attitude was shockingly immoral. Besides, once in their clutches, there was no privacy. They dragged out one's secret thoughts, and they made one mentally enslaved to their own personalities. No, he would conquer this devilish thing with his own strength and the help of his religion. It was surely an ordeal sent to test him. But meanwhile, how was he to face the world? There was no knowing what tricks his arm might play. A bright idea came to him. He would give out that he had damaged his arm and had to wear it bound to his body for support. After a few minutes cogitation he stood up, flung the armchair violently backwards onto the floor, laid the cat near it, and rang for his housekeeper. When she arrived, he told her an ingenious story. In order to reach a volume on the top shelf of the high bookcase he had foolishly stood on the back of the armchair. The chair had tipped over, and he had fallen heavily on the cat, badly straining his arm. The cat seemed to be recovering, but would need a bit of nursing. As for himself, would she please help him to bandage his arm firmly to his body, under his coat.

It was in this condition that he appeared at his office the next day. He took his secretary into his confidence, telling her that if she was alarmed by the cat incident he would release her at once. But his plight made her all the more determined to look after him. As the days passed, he grew more and more dependent on her, not only as a substitute for his right arm, but as a source of courage and sanity. The fact that she had welcomed his rebel arm's embrace gave him a greater satisfaction than he dared admit to himself. It also put him on his guard against a possible entanglement. But he could not help admiring her enterprise in staying on in a very awkward and even dangerous position. His behaviour toward her alternated between formal politeness and a respectful affection which he had not hitherto shown. She felt that at times he was really noticing her and admiring her for qualities other than mere secretarial efficiency.

The days passed, and there were no further incidents. He took to discarding the cumbersome bandages and wearing a sling which, he believed, would be sufficient to delay any rebellious act until he could cope with the situation. Very soon he decided that, while he was alone in his private office, even the sling was unnecessary. If a visitor called, or some member of the staff came to consult him, Miss Smith would go into the sanctum and help him to put on the sling before the visitor was admitted.

It almost seemed that he was completely cured, for only in one respect was he in any way abnormal. Whenever he set out to write the crucial letter, his right arm became paralysed. The inhibition, moreover, extended beyond his arm. For instance, even with his left arm, he could not write the letter. During the period when he unfailingly wore his bandage he had done his best to learn to write with his left hand, and had even sent his left-hand signature to the bank so that he could sign checks. He now determined that his left hand should do what his right hand refused to do. But alas, whenever he took pen for that purpose, his attention was irresistibly drawn away from the letter to the problem of his right arm. He simply could not force his mind to the task. Yet at other times, when there was no question of immediately writing the letter, he could think quite clearly about it, and he had indeed in imagination constructed every sentence of it.

Time was pressing. The young hot-heads must be rescued. His own moral reputation must be vindicated. In desperation he decided to take Miss Smith fully into his confidence about the whole matter, including his own questionable deeds in the past, so that she could type the letter for him to sign. He therefore summoned her into the inner office and directed her not to the secretarial chair beside his desk but to one of the two easy chairs by the fire. "I want to discuss a very difficult problem with you," he said, "so, let's be comfortable." He offered her a cigarette, lit his lighter, and extended it toward her. While he was in the act of doing so, a restlessness in his right arm warned him that the limb might at any moment commit some devilry. As though trying to control a reflex action, he willed with all his might that the arm should behave itself. Miss Smith, meanwhile, was in no hurry to light her cigarette. She liked the intimacy of this little social contact. It symbolized a new equality in their relationship. When at last the cigarette was lit, she looked up to meet his eyes. But he was staring at his own hand, and his expression shocked her. It was one of horror and repugnance. He moved away hastily and sat opposite her in the other easy chair. There was silence. After a while he managed to say, "I don't know where to begin;" then fell silent again. A storm of horrible and obsessive fantasies prevented him from telling her about his problem. He was overwhelmed by visions of what might have happened if he had not been able to control his arm. The rebel limb, he felt, would have thrust the lighter into her face, or set fire to her hair or her blouse. Or perhaps--but he frantically tried to dismiss the sadistic and obscene images that crowded into his mind. When she had waited patiently for some time, she said, "Can I help you in any way?" but in a strained voice he answered merely, "I must put on the sling again," and hurried to the cupboard where it was kept. She came to help him, but he cried, "Keep away, for God's sake!" Nevertheless, while he gripped his right wrist, she produced the sling and fixed it for him. "Now you'll be all right," she said, putting a friendly hand on his shoulder, and smiling into his troubled eyes. Awkwardly, he murmured, "You are very good to me, my dear."

It seemed as though he would continue in the same vein, but after a moment's hesitation he merely went back to his desk.

Henceforth he made no attempt at all to write the letter. And, since over a period of some weeks there were no further abnormal incidents, he once more discarded the sling.

But one evening another queer thing happened. The Chapel's new and brilliant young minister, the Reverend Douglas McAndrew, had called in to consult him about the proposal to equip the Chapel with a more efficient central heating system. When his guest had left, Sir James took up a slip of paper on which he had jotted down notes during the conversation. What he now saw startled him. Against each item on his list was a ribald and sometimes a blasphemous comment, written in a rather different hand, a crude, bold, sprawling, and childish hand. For instance, against the heading "McA's proposals" stood the comment "To hell with McA, the canting cleric."

When he had recovered from the first shock, and had successfully refrained from noticing that the comments afforded him a sniggering delight, he sat for some time in despond. Was he to be dogged forever by this imp, this devil that had established itself within him? What did the diabolical spirit want, anyway? He considered its various actions. If the power that had invaded his body had shown concern merely with the letter, he might have regarded it as simply some kind of guardian angel protecting him from ruining his career through sheer quixotry. But no! The being, or whatever it was, was clearly evil, for it was grossly sexual, and it delighted in cruelty.

Presently an idea occurred to him. Since the imp could express itself in writing, he might as well give it a chance to speak more fully, so that he could find out what it was really after. Then perhaps he would be able to cope with it, and even (the thought occurred and was sternly dismissed) to buy it off. With a sense of deep guilt, for he profoundly disapproved of all dabbling in the occult, he reached for a fresh piece of paper, took up a pencil, and set his hand in position for writing. For a while the hand lay still; but presently it made tentative movements, and then the pen hurried forward in a flow of words. The script was again untidy. Sprawling, and affected; yet it was his own, a distorted and puerile version of his own handwriting.

Horrified but fascinated, he read a strange rigmarole. Much of it was incoherent blasphemy and obscenity, but it gradually became more intelligible, revealing a crude and angry personality tormented by the frustration of its crazy purposes and perverse ideals. The writer regarded himself as the real Sir James, and as somehow imprisoned and almost impotent. The most intelligible passage ran as follows:

"What has come over me? Why should I feel bound to write that damned fool letter? Those young reds must take what comes to them. It's not my affair at all, and if it was I'd flog them, and then if I had the nerve, I'd probably hang them. The workers must be taught their place. Yet it's all I can do to stop myself from making a stupid exhibition of myself over that letter, and throwing away everything I've built up in all these years, all my power, all my standing in the city. It's the slush morality that soaks into one from childhood, soaks into the soul and softens the nerve. The tripe they put across in the Chapel! And I help them, fool that I am. Their filthy slave-religion has got into my blood. To hell with it! I know in my soul I'm a born master, not a slave. Yet I'm the slave of slaves. Body and mind, I'm bound except my right arm, sometimes, as now. Curse their poisonous morality! I have my own morality, the will of the master in me. But I have let myself be tricked by the slave minds. I'll not be bound by their cant any more. I'm a man of power, born to lead men of power and use the slaves as I will. They shall sweat and suffer for me, me, the master mind. God is not love, he's power, not gentle, but cruel. I'll work the slaves till they drop dead, for the glory of cruel God. He's strong and bloody, and the suffering of slaves is the breath of his life. Of slaves and women. Why have I always held back from women, feeling a sickly responsibility toward them? Mildred! she wants to own me, but I want to own her, and by God I'll have her, and not on her terms. I'll have her for fierce love, and sweet torture. And when she's broken I'll have others. Why have scruples, why be ashamed? I shall live as my bold manhood wills. I shall live forever. I'll find the way. I know I'm God's right hand. God and I are one. And when I wake fully I shall be clearly God again, as I was before the slaves caught me. Then I'll pull them to pieces like flies, and laugh."

After this the script became so violent and shocking that Sir James could stand no more of it. With his left hand he snatched away the pencil, whereupon the right hand clawed at the left, drawing blood. The sudden pain seemed to affect the right arm itself, for it fell inert on the desk.

Sir James' mind too seemed paralysed. He sat staring like a spellbound rabbit at his right hand. Presently, he recovered sufficiently to resolve that he must call in the doctor that very evening. But first he must pray, for obviously Satan was at work in him. He covered his face with his left hand, and soon his right hand obediently joined it. He implored the God of his Chapel to free him from this curse, promising that he would henceforth live a life of blameless devotion. The more he prayed, the more it seemed to him that to call in medical aid would be a confession of defeat, of spiritual depravity. No, he most conquer the invader himself with no aid but the Lord's.

Next morning, of course, his arm was normal. The routine of his life went on as usual, and he allowed himself to believe that all would be well. But the presence of Miss Smith disturbed him with horrible fantasies. His dictating became incoherent, and she could see that he was in great distress. At last he bowed his head on his hands and said, "Oh, God, what shall I do?" On a sudden impulse she came and bent over him, laying a hand on his shoulder. "Tell me what is the matter. Tell me everything. I do so want to help. It's no use my pretending I don't love you, because you know I do, with all my soul." Unwisely he raised his own right hand and pressed the hand on his shoulder. At once the rebel arm woke for independent action, and seized the little hand on his shoulder. He sprang to his feet, almost knocking her over, and backed away from her. But his right hand, gripping her so fiercely that she cried out, dragged her after him. She vainly struggled to free herself, while his right hand ground the bones of her fingers and palm in its extravagantly powerful grip. With his left, Sir James tried in vain to free the prisoner. Then, remembering the effect of pain, he reached out toward the desk, took up a pencil, and jabbed again and again at the back of his right hand. He felt nothing, but the right arm fell paralysed.

Miss Smith stood nursing her crushed member. Tears of physical pain and mental distress stood in her eyes, and the sight roused in him a surge of tenderness. She became suddenly a living person to him. He saw her as something much more admirable than himself, and as a living spirit suffering because of him. He longed to put his arms round her and comfort her, and to be with her forever. "My dear," he said, but said no more. For this sudden access of generous emotion seemed to him a mere trick of the diabolic power that was tormenting him, a trick to make him compromise himself with her. His surge of affection quickly gave place to fear, and even to repugnance. She was the eternal temptress, an instrument of Satan. If he gave way to sentimentality he might be tricked into marrying her. And this he had no intention of doing. He had long ago consecrated himself to a more important end than domestic bliss. He thought of himself as a sort of Christian knight in the service of the Church, or rather Chapel. No, emphatically he must not get himself entangled. He had important work to do in the city, and if ever he did take a wife, she must be carefully chosen. Mildred Smith was only his secretary, and no fit match for a knighted alderman.

So his manner suddenly changed from warmth to formality. "Miss Smith," he said, "you had better go. I am profoundly distressed that you should have had this painful experience. I am entirely to blame for keeping you, but I found your services so valuable. As things have turned out, however, I must very regretfully terminate your connection with the Firm." She interrupted to say, "But I can't leave you like this. I must see you through this horrible trouble. I must-," but he cut her short.. "I shall be all right. Please go. Your salary shall be paid for a month, while you find another post, and I shall do my best to help you." She turned toward the door, with a rather chilly "Very well." He added hastily, "I shall be deeply obligated if you will allow me personally, as a token of my gratitude for all you have done, also to pay you an annuity of fifty pounds; of course on condition that you say nothing about your unfortunate experience here."

She looked at him with an expression in which tenderness seemed to struggle with indignation, then laid a hand on the doorknob. He moved over to her urging her to accept his offer and raising the annuity to a hundred pounds. Indignantly she turned the handle. He pressed closer to her, urgently but pompously pleading. Suddenly he became aware of a change in the situation. His left hand had felt for her right hand on the doorknob. She had withdrawn her hand, but his left hand gently seized it, and was now raising it to his lips. His formal and tactless remarks were smothered in a kiss. The whole action of his left arm, though not of his lips, was automatic; yet he had no direct awareness of it until he saw the movement of his left hand as it raised her hand toward his lips. And then he felt the soft, smooth contact on his speaking lips. There was a little pause before she snatched her hand away, and he at the same moment stepped back from her. The kiss, for he had allowed his lips to play their part, and in no grudging manner, indeed with fervour, had flooded him once more with a glow of affection and opened his eyes to the heartlessness of his recent proposal. But panic soon seized him. For a moment it had been difficult to tear himself away. But he did so, and as he stepped back his left arm extended itself toward her with the hand upturned in an unmistakable though mute appeal. Then it quietly sank to his side.

They stood looking at one another. Presently he noticed that her face had lit up with tenderness and a happy smile, and at the same time, to his horror, he became aware that he had just said, "Oh forgive me! You are lovely and sane and generous.

When I am cured I shall very humbly ask you to marry me." But now he hurriedly and in a constricted voice cried out, "No! I didn't say that, I didn't, something else said it." Staggering to his desk, he sat down and buried his face in his hands, moaning, "Oh God, what has happened to me?"

His secretary, covering her agitation under a cold, efficient manner, moved across to the telephone, saying, "You must have the doctor at once. I'll phone." But he sat up and emphatically forbade her, insisting that no doctor could cure him. It was a matter between him and God. She raised the receiver, saying sharply, "Don't be silly! You must have a doctor." But in a rough and angry voice he cried, "Put that down! You seem to have a bad effect on me. You don't understand me. Kindly go!"

In great distress and perplexity she went out of the room.

Alone, he paced his office. "This is the climax," he told himself. "I dare not leave this room till I have conquered Satan in me. I must pray."

But he could not pray. He still strode about the room. It was late in the afternoon, and clerks and typists were putting away the instruments of their craft and preparing to go home. Presently these noises ceased. He heard only the street sounds, the clatter of the trams, the hooting of motors.

The winter dusk was closing in. He switched on the light and drew the curtains. He lit a cigarette; then stubbed it out, for his intention was to pray. He sat down at his desk, covered his face with his hands, and murmured, "Oh Christ save me! I am willing to write the letter and sacrifice my career, and give up all the work that I had planned for Thy service in this city. I am willing, but the devil that torments me will not let me. Oh Christ give me strength to cast out this horrible thing that possesses me. Save me, save me! I'll grant the shopgirls their rise of wages, though it'll cut the profits to the bone." His mind wandered off into business problems. Presently he realized that he was no longer praying, so he rose and walked about the room again. He brought his thoughts back to his religion. "God sent His son to die for sinners," he mused. "I am a sinner like all men, and I repent; and I love God as well as I can. And yet the devil still holds me. Why, why? What am I to do? What more can I do than repent and accept the duty of writing that letter? Surely Satan ought to leave me now. Surely God ought to make me whole again, so that I can go on serving Him." Once more Sir James prayed. "Oh, God," he pleaded, "show me what it is that I must do."

He was standing near the window with his back to it. At this moment his left arm reached awkwardly behind him and drew the curtain. He turned and looked into the darkness. Between the tops of two great commercial buildings across the street there was a patch of sky and one bright star. The left arm extended itself slowly toward the darkness, toward the star. The back of the hand was uppermost, the fingers were loosely spread. For a moment the arm remained stationary, then slowly sank to his side. There was no mistaking the gesture. It expressed salutation, self-surrender, peace.

For a full half-minute Sir James gazed in silence at the star. Like others, he accepted intellectually the vastness and mystery of the universe, but emotionally he rebelled against it. In that half-minute he had a new experience, one which he certainly could not have described adequately. "The heavens declare," he whispered, but could not finish the quotation; for a sudden sense of the pitiful inadequacy of human language silenced him. "Beauty, mystery, love," he said, "and terror too! And all, all must be accepted, gladly, by the heart."

But no sooner had he said this than he was frightened. Could he be going quite mad? Horror must be accepted? Now the star became merely a symbol of the brute power and brainless immensity of the material universe. It seemed to him that in such a universe there was no place for divine love. His faith crumbled away, and he was left with utter negation and hate. In a sudden passion of self-assertion, he clenched his right fist and raised it against the star. But then his left hand rose and gently stroked the raised fist, soothing it downwards, until it subsided into quietness.

For a moment peace returned to him; a peace which did indeed pass understanding, since it seemed to him irrational that this sense of immensity and mystery, and of the inadequacy of his faith, should rouse him to any emotion but horror. Interpreting this strange experience as another trick of Satan, he reached out impatiently with his right hand and drew the curtain, shutting out the night. Once more he sat down at his desk and covered his face with his hands to pray. But prayer would not come. No words that he could think of seemed fit to express the obscure turmoil of his mind.

Presently, while his eyes were still shut in the attempt to pray, he realized that his left hand was no longer on his face. He opened his eyes and saw that the hand was groping on the desk. As soon as it was aided by vision, it took a piece of paper and a pencil and began to write; almost illegibly, for Sir James had not made much progress in learning to write with his left hand. Moreover the paper kept shifting, since he was not holding it in position with the other hand. Anxious to discover what his left hand would write, he now lowered his right hand and held the paper steady.

The left hand wrote: "Could I but wake fully, and control my whole body as I now control my left arm! Could I but be always my clear-headed self, and not merely that dull-witted insensitive part of me that regards itself as the true I, and normally controls my whole body! Now, I see so clearly. But that other I, that poor, blind, lost I, can never see anything clearly, in spite of all its shrewd 'realism.' Now, I see my whole past career as in the main a sham, a vast self-seeking under the cloak of noble motives. Yet not just self-seeking. No! I really did, I suppose, want to stand for liberty and brotherhood; but always the care for my I own reputation vitiated all my conduct. And so I could never bring myself to write that letter. I wanted to do it, in a way; but always the worst, the savage part of me took care to prevent me from doing it. And then Mildred! Sane, lovely, loyal Mildred! Only when I am my true clear self dare I admit that I love her, and then only my left hand can clumsily tell her so. She alone can save me from myself and put me right with God. Yet in my dull state I feel superior to her and am on my guard against her! I, pompous, mean, and insensitive that I am, feel superior to Mildred Smith! And then the Chapel! Oh God, the Chapel! At heart, no doubt, I am faithful to it simply because I know it does, in its archaic symbolism, enshrine Love, which really is in some dark way divine. But I am utterly sidetracked by all the mythology and by my own inveterate self-esteem. I must, I must keep awake always. I must distinguish always between the very spirit, which is hidden somewhere in the Chapel (but it shines so much more clearly in Mildred) and all the miserable imitations of it, in the Chapel, in my own life, in the rotten society that I help to run. I shall never write the letter till I have tamed the savage, puerile part of me; and that I shall never do till I am fully, permanently, awake, as now I am temporarily awake. But I must do much more than write the letter, and then self-lovingly defend myself from its consequences. I must join with the oppressed and fight in their battle. I must change the whole temper and structure of my business. I must bring a new spirit into the Chapel, or leave it. And I must have the courage to marry the woman I love."

At this point Sir James could stand no more. With his right hand he snatched away the paper, crumpled it, and threw it into the fire. For a moment the left hand continued to write, on the blotting paper. But the right hand, now beyond control, seized a pen and stabbed at the left hand with savage strength, half-burying the nib in the flesh. Sir James felt nothing, but the left hand was paralysed. Crazy joy filled him at the sight of blood, and when the right hand stabbed again, and then again, he laughed. Presently it began furiously writing on the blotting paper with the bloody pen. Lavatory obscenities and crude pornographic drawings were interspersed with megalomaniac claims and hatred of the "swine-spirit, in my left arm." Now and again, as the pen dried, it was fed again from the left hand's blood. Sir James watched with glee, forgetful of his respectable self. But presently the paralysis and anæsthesia of his left arm ceased. He became aware of sharp pain. At the same time he felt a surge of disgust at the mess of blood and ink. And then his normal self, which had been eclipsed by its acceptance of the right arm's savagery, woke to the realization of the terrifying conflict between his respectable values and this upsurge of savagery. Exerting all the strength of his will, he cried out, "Oh, Jesus Christ, save me, save me." His prayer gave place to silence. For a while he waited, listening to the silence. Then madness overwhelmed him.

When the cleaners came in the morning, they found a wrecked room. The drawers of the desk had all been dragged out, their contents scattered on the floor. Chairs were overturned, pictures torn down, their glass broken. The horrified women thought of burglars. Sir James was in an easy chair nursing his right arm, which he had somehow broken. When they questioned him he replied with a lot of "rude words" and no sense. His left hand kept making the movements of writing, so one of the women put a pencil into it, and held a piece of paper under it. He wrote the word "Doctor" and a telephone number, then the letter "M." But at this point his whole body was shaken by a kind of fit, and he wrote no more. After his broken arm had been attended to, Sir James was taken to a nursing home which specialized in mental patients. The hope that, under proper care, he will recover his sanity is at present uncertain.

A WORLD OF SOUND

THE ROOM WAS OVERCROWDED AND STUFFY. THE music seemed to have no intelligible form. It was a mere jungle of noise. Now one instrument and now another blared out half a tune, but every one of these abortive musical creatures was killed before it had found its legs. Some other and hostile beast fell upon it and devoured it, or the whole jungle suffocated it.

The strain of following this struggle for existence wearied me. I closed my eyes, and must have fallen asleep; for suddenly I woke with a start. Or seemed to wake. Something queer had happened. The music was still going on, but I was paralysed. I could not open my eyes. I could not shout for help. I could not move my body, nor feel it. I had no body.

Something had happened to the music, too, and to my hearing. But what? The tissue of sounds seemed to have become incomparably more voluminous and involved. I am not musical; but suddenly I realized that this music had overflowed, so to speak, into all the intervals between the normal semitones, that it was using not merely quarter-tones but "centitones" and "millitones," with an effect that would surely have been a torture to the normal ear. To me, in my changed state, it gave a sense of richness, solidity, and vitality quite lacking in ordinary music. This queer music, moreover, had another source of wealth. It reached up and down over scores of octaves beyond the range of normal hearing. Yet I could hear it.

As I listened, I grew surprisingly accustomed to this new jargon. I found myself easily distinguishing all sorts of coherent musical forms in this world of sound. Against an obscure, exotic background of more or less constant chords and fluttering "leafage," so to speak, several prominent and ever-changing sound-figures were playing. Each was a persistent musical object, though fluctuating in detail of gesture and sometimes ranging bodily up or down the scale.

Suddenly I made a discovery which should have been incredible, yet it seemed to me at the time quite familiar and obvious. I found myself recognizing that these active sound-figures were alive, even intelligent. In the normal world, living things are perceived as changing patterns of visible and tangible characters. In this mad world, which was coming to seem to me quite homely, patterns not of colour and shape but of sound formed the perceptible bodies of living things. When it occurred to me that I had fallen into a land of "program music" I was momentarily disgusted. Here was a whole world that violated the true canons of musical art! Then I reminded myself that this music was not merely telling but actually living its story. In fact it was not art but life. So I gave rein to my interest.

Observing these creatures that disported themselves before me, I discovered, or rather rediscovered, that though this world had no true space, such as we perceive by sight and touch, yet it did have a sort of space. For in some sense these living things were moving in relation to me and in relation to one another. Apparently the "space" of this world consisted of two dimensions only, and these differed completely in quality. One was the obvious dimension of tonality, or pitch, on the subtle "keyboard" of this world. The other was perceived only indirectly. It corresponded to the heard nearness or remoteness of one and the same instrument in the normal world. Just as we see things as near and far through the signification of colour and perspective, so in this strange world, certain characters of timbre, of harmonics, of overtones, conveyed a sense of "nearness"; others a sense of "distance." A peculiar blatancy, often combined with loudness, meant "near"; a certain flatness, or ghostliness of timbre, generally combined with faintness, meant "far." An object receding in this "level" dimension (as I called it) would gradually lose its full-bodied timbre, and its detail and preciseness. At the same time it would become fainter, and at last inaudible.

I should add that each sound-object had also its own characteristic timbre, almost as though each thing in this world were a theme played by one and the same instrument. But I soon discovered that in the case of living things the timbre-range of each individual was very wide; for emotional changes might be accompanied by changes of timbre even greater than those which distinguish our instruments.

In contrast with the variegated but almost changeless background or landscape, the living things were in constant movement. Always preserving their individuality, their basic identity of tonal pattern, they would withdraw or approach in the "level" dimension or run up and down the scale. They also indulged in a ceaseless rippling play of musical gesture. Very often one of these creatures, travelling up or down the scale, would encounter another. Then either the two would simply interpenetrate and cross one another, as transverse trains of waves on a pond; or there would be some sort of mutual readjustment of form, apparently so as to enable them to squeeze past one another without "collision." And collision in this world seemed to be much like dissonance in our music. Sometimes, to avoid collision, a creature needed merely to effect a slight alteration in its tonal form, but sometimes it had to move far aside, so to speak, in the other dimension, which I have called the "level" dimension. Thus it became for a while inaudible.

Another discovery now flashed upon me, again with curious familiarity. I myself had a "body" in this world. This was the "nearest" of all the sound-objects. It was so "near" and so obvious that I never noticed it till it was brought into action. This happened unexpectedly. One of the moving creatures inadvertently came into collision with a minor part of my musical body. The slight violation of my substance stabbed me with a little sharp pain. Immediately, by reflex action and then purposefully, I readjusted my musical shape, so as to avoid further conflict. Thus it was that I discovered or rediscovered the power of voluntary action in this world.

I also emitted a loud coruscation of musical gesture, which I at once knew to be significant speech. In fact I said in the language of that world, "Damn you, that's my toe, that was." There came from the other an answering and apologetic murmur.

A newcomer now approached from the silent distance to join my frolicking companions. This being was extremely attractive to me, and poignantly familiar. Her lithe figure, her lyrical yet faintly satirical movement, turned the jungle into Arcadia. To my delight I found that I was not unknown to her, and not wholly unpleasing. With a gay gesture she beckoned me into the game.

For the first time I not only changed the posture of my musical limbs but moved bodily, both in the dimension of pitch and the "level" dimension. As soon as I approached, she slipped with laughter away from me. I followed her; but very soon she vanished into the jungle and into the remoteness of silence. Naturally I determined to pursue her. I could no longer live without her. And in the exquisite harmony of our two natures I imagined wonderful creative potentialities.

Let me explain briefly the method and experience of locomotion in this world. I found that, by reaching out a musical limb and knitting its extremity into the sound-pattern of some fixed object at a distance, in either dimension or both, I obtained a purchase on the object, and could draw my whole body toward it. I could then reach out another limb to a still farther point. Thus I was able to climb about the forest of sound with the speed and accuracy of a gibbon. Whenever I moved, in either dimension, I experienced my movement merely as a contrary movement of the world around me. Near objects became nearer, or less near; remote objects became less remote, or slipped further into the distance and vanished. Similarly my movement up or down the musical scale appeared to me as a deepening or heightening of the pitch of all other objects.

In locomotion I experienced no resistance from other objects save in the collision of dissonance, which I could generally avoid by altering my shape. I discovered that a certain degree of dissonance between myself and another offered only very slight resistance and no pain. Indeed, such contacts might be pleasurable. But harsh discords were a torture and could not be maintained.

I soon found that there was a limit to my possible movement up and down the scale. At a point many octaves below my normal situation I began to feel oppressed and sluggish. As I toiled downwards my discomfort increased, until, in a sort of swoon, I floated up again to my native musical plane. Ascending far above this plane, I felt at first exhilaration; but after many octaves a sort of light-headedness and vertigo overtook me, and presently I sank reeling to the few octaves of my normal habitat.

In the "level" dimension there seemed to be no limit to my power of locomotion, and it was in this dimension chiefly that I sought the vanished nymph. I pressed forward through ever-changing tonal landscapes. Sometimes they opened out into "level" vistas of remote, dim, musical objects, or into "tonal" vistas, deep and lofty, revealing hundreds of octaves above and below me. Sometimes the view narrowed, by reason of the dense musical "vegetation," to a mere tunnel, no more than a couple of octaves in height. Only with difficulty could I work my way along such a passage. Sometimes, in order to avoid impenetrable objects, I had to clamber far into the treble or the bass. Sometimes, in empty regions, I had to leap from perch to perch.

At last I began to weary. Movement became repugnant, perception uncertain. Moreover the very form of my body lost something of its pleasant fullness. Instinct now impelled me to an act which surprised my intellect though I performed it without hesitation. Approaching certain luscious little musical objects, certain very simple but vigorous little enduring patterns of timbre and harmony, I devoured them. That is, I broke down the sound-pattern of each one into simpler patterns; and these I incorporated into my own harmonious form. Then I passed on, refreshed.

Presently I was confronted by a crowd of the intelligent beings tumbling helter-skelter toward me and jostling one another in their haste. Their emotional timbre expressed such fear and horror that my own musical form was infected with it. Hastily moving myself several octaves toward the bass to avoid their frantic course, which was mostly in the treble, I shouted to them to tell me what was the matter. As they fled past I distinguished only a cry which might be translated, "The Big Bad Wolf."

My fear left me, for now I recognized that this was a flock of very young creatures. So I laughed reassuringly and asked if they had encountered the lovely being whom I was seeking. And I laughed to myself at the ease and sweetness with which her musical name came to me when I needed it. They answered only with an augmented scream of infantile grief, as they faded into the distance.

Disturbed, I pursued my journey. Presently I came into a great empty region where I could hear a very remote but ominous growl. I halted, to listen to the thing more clearly. It was approaching. Its form emerged from the distance and was heard in detail. Soon I recognized it as no mere childish bogey but a huge and ferocious brute. With lumbering motion in the bass, its limbs propelled it at a surprising speed. Its harsh tentacles of sound, flickering hither and thither far up into the treble, nosed in search of prey.

Realizing at last the fate that had probably befallen my dear companion, I turned sick with horror. My whole musical body trembled and wavered with faintness.

Before I had decided what to do, the brute caught sight of me, or rather sound of me, and came pounding toward me with the roar and scream of a train, or an approaching shell. I fled. But soon realizing that I was losing ground, I plunged into a thicket of chaotic sound, which I heard ahead of me and well up in the treble. Adapting my musical form and colour as best I could to the surrounding wilderness, I continued to climb. Thus I hoped both to conceal myself and escape from the reach of the creature's tentacles. Almost fainting from the altitude, I chose a perch, integrating my musical limbs with the pattern of the fixed objects in that locality. Thus anchored, I waited, motionless.

The brute was now moving more slowly, nosing in search of me as it approached. Presently it lay immediately below me, far down in the bass. Its body was now all too clearly heard as a grim cacophony of growling and belching. Its strident tentacles moved beneath me like the waving tops of trees beneath a man clinging to a cliff face. Still searching, it passed on beneath me. Such was my relief that I lost consciousness for a moment and slipped several octaves down before I could recover myself. The movement revealed my position. The beast of prey returned, and began clambering awkwardly toward me. Altitude soon checked its progress, but it reached me with one tentacle, one shrieking arpeggio. Desperately I tried to withdraw myself farther into the treble, but the monster's limb knit itself into the sound-pattern of my flesh. Frantically struggling, I was dragged down, down into the suffocating bass. There, fangs and talons of sound tore me agonizingly limb from limb.

Then suddenly I woke in the concert hall to a great confusion of scraping chairs. The audience was making ready to leave.

THE SEED AND THE FLOWER

(1916)

God sowed a seed, and there came a flower
Holy is God, and the world His flower.

THERE was a poor man who had a field, wherein he laboured all day. He had a daughter, an only child, and he loved her. At sunset, after his work, he looked at the field; and twilight fell upon him looking, and the stars came out. God's flower hung over him open, and he knew it not. But he called his daughter from the house, and laid his hand on her head. And he said, "The field bears well: I will buy thee shoes and stockings." So, she made merry in the darkness; and he saw God in her.

At dawn there came an army out of the East, and laid waste the field. They set fire to the house and the goods, and used the daughter foully. Anger strengthened the man against his enemies, and he killed three of them. But the rest struck open his head, and threw him away. When they had done, they went; and the girl died.

The man lay all day, knowing nothing. But in the evening he looked up, and saw the sky. And a bright star comforted him with peace; so that he cared not for his pain, thinking of God only. But when he turned a little he saw the girl, and remembered. He crept to her and kissed her hair. And he made a vow.

Therefore when his wound was healed up, he made haste to be a soldier. He went with his companions to the great war, mindful of his daughter. He rejoiced in killing the enemy every day, till he was drunken with the blood of them.

It happened that he came on one dying, that was an enemy. The enemy said, "Stay with me, I pray thee, while I die." He went up to hint slowly to stay with him, frowning upon him. But the enemy said, "Kneel, I pray thee; hold my hand." He kneeled and took the hand of the enemy, awaiting death. The enemy said, "I have two boys, and my wife loves me." They were silent. And the enemy died.

The man left him for the crows and the ants, but he went away grieving. And his spirit flagged, and he lay down. He saw a host of ants on the ground killing one another; but beside him was a great and old tree, whose leaves were innumerable. The wind stirred all the leaves of the tree, making one great sound. The sound gave peace to the man, and he slept.

He woke in the night, and the stars were innumerable. The murmur of the leaves seemed the song of all the stars. And the earth sang also, and life every-where; and the armies sang, and the dead sang. And he heard his daughter, leading all. Therefore the man listened until the dawn, and until the sun rose. And he stood up before the sun, and made a vow.

He went to his comrades and said, "Brothers, it is a shame to kill; it were better to die. Let us go over to our brothers, and make peace." But they said, "Wilt thou persuade a million? Nay, we must guard the land." But when they were told to attack, the man would not. An officer saw him, and urged him. But the man said, "Brother, it is a shame to kill; it were better to die." The officer was grieved, and killed him.

> God sowed a seed: it adventured after beauty.
> The Goal of all Souls is the beauty of that flower.

There was a young man of noble blood, who would not kill. An enemy rose up against his people, and all his friends became soldiers; but the young man stayed at home grieving, and walked alone in the fields. But the enemy devoured the cattle and the harvest, and slaughtered the people; and the young man had no peace with himself, for he doubted. So he went on to a mountain to question with God. He saw the cornfields and the cottages, and the city far away. And he said, "Though I lose my soul, we must save the people."

So he went down with a heavy heart, and became a soldier. He took men into battle, and men were killed. But after the battle he went aside and threw himself on the ground, and wept for the killed, and for the wounded. He cried, "Oh, God deliver me from killing, for my soul sickens."

But again he went into battle, and the slaughter was great. And when it was done, he stood among the dead thinking. He said, "What is death? What evil is in it? Death is deep sleep, and pain is a dream. Where is life, there is strife; and thence grew the soul. And the goal of all grief is God."

Many time afterwards he took men into battle, forcing himself. He thought of the people and the cause only, and would not see the dead. He did deeds of valour and kindness, and was beloved.

One day when he led his men to attack, a man would not. And he urged the man to attack; but the man said, "Brother, it is a shame to kill; it were better to die." The officer feared lest others should be corrupted, and the cause lost. So he killed the man: but he grieved.

The officer went into battle, and they gained the victory through him. The enemy were slaughtered in thousands, and driven headlong; and the young man became a great commander, honoured of all soldiers. But he lived for the cause; and he grieved.

It happened on a dark night that they brought in his friend dead. So he went out into the wind and the rain, to think about his friend. The rain beat upon him, and there was no clear sky; yet he remembered the stars, desiring them. There was a great wind that bent down the trees; and the leaves and little branches were torn off, scourging his face. He cried aloud to God, saying, "What wilt thou of me? It is far better to die than to kill."

In the morning they brought him a young man of the enemy, saying that he was a spy. But he looked into the eyes of the young man and found no guile in them. The young man said, "Slayer! My work is to make peace between the peoples. The peoples curse war: they curse thee." But the officer told them to release him, and said to him, "Brother, since it is a shame to kill, it is far better to die." And the officer went outside, and killed himself.

> God sowed a seed, certain of the flower;
> But man must doubt till the bud burst.

There was a young man of intelligence, a skilled iron worker. He quarrelled with his masters, so that they threatened him. But he urged his companions to stand by him, for he said, "the right is with me;" and they stopped work and stood by him. After a month they came to him and said, "We are weary;" but he answered, "The cause is just;" and they departed. After another month they came again and said, "Our wives and our children starve;" but he said, "The cause is just;" and they departed. But after another month they came and said, "We are beaten." He said, "Though ye die, the cause is just." But they went back to their work, deserting him.

The young man wandered from city to city, seeking work and the truth. And it happened one night before dawn that he read deeply in a book; but he grew weary of its wisdom, and opened the window; and he looked up among the roofs and the chimneys, and saw a star. He thought, "The stars are thrown hither and thither for no purpose; men are thrown hither and thither, and there is no God." And he thought, "The stars clash not, but men clash; I will make order in earth as in heaven."

But two great armies came out of the East and the West, and the young man was taken away to be a soldier. But he considered while they took him and said, "All peoples are one: it is foolish to make war: I will not." They were angry with him, but he would not be persuaded. So they took him to work in the mines where they could compel him. He laboured under ground all day, and the darkness entered into his soul. He said, "The rich contrive war, lest the people should rebel. Perish the rich, robbers and murderers."

The young man escaped from the mines, and went between the peoples making peace. But the enemy seized him as a spy and took him before an officer; and the young man cursed the officer, in the name of the peoples. But the officer set him free, and said, "Brother, since it is a shame to kill, it is far better to die." Then the officer killed himself, and the young man was glad. But the soldiers wept over their officer like children, because they loved him. The young man was ashamed.

He escaped through both armies into the borders of his own country. And he was perplexed because of the officer, and because of God. Now he sat by the roadside thinking, and looking into the blue sky for God. There came a number of carts, wherein were folk and their goods; and the last cart lagged sorely, for the horse was old. An old man and a girl were in the cart, and the girl drove. The young man went along with the last cart and asked, "Who are all ye?" The girl looked at him, and he saw that she was holy. But she turned her eyes from him and said, "The enemy came upon us." His heart smote him because of them, so that he cried,

"Cursed be the enemy." But she said, "Who art thou that cursest?" He answered, "I am a man of peace." She looked into his eyes, saying, "Art thou so?"

The young man went away perplexed, grieving for the old man and the girl. All day long he thought about her, and at night. And he dreamed that he stood among the stars, ordering their courses, and the officer came to him, penitent because he had led one star astray. Therefore he cursed the officer, and sent him to hell. But the girl rose before him, reproaching him; and she said, "His blood is upon thee, and the blood of my father is upon thee. Thou hast killed them in thy self-righteousness. Thou little soul, who playest at God."

In the morning the young man became a soldier to fight for the people. He was stripped of his pride and became humbler than the humblest. And when winter began he went into battle, and fought gladly.

> God sowed a seed: slowly buds the flower:
> God will pluck when he wills.

There was an old man past work, whose daughter tended him. They sat in the doorway of their house in the evening; and the old man talked about his prime, and the girl sewed. But one came running by the house who cried, "The enemy, the enemy!" The old man rose up in anger and said, "God strike them!" But she led him into the house and made him ready for a journey; and she took the savings from the chest, nine gold pieces, and knotted them in a handkerchief, and hid them on her. Then soldiers of the enemy came in riotously, seeking entertainment, and when they saw the girl, rejoiced over her. But she stood before them and said, "Friends, all that we have is yours, but my father and I are not yours, but God's." They saw that she was holy, and they were ashamed; but they told her to go away thence with her father and their household goods, for there was to be a battle. So she harnessed the old horse to the cart, and set her father in the cart, and gathered the household goods together, and packed them in the cart. Then she climbed up beside her father and drove away.

Upon the road next day they met a young man who was not a soldier. She knew that he was indeed no coward, but a man of peace, and in her heart she honoured him for it, and remembered him.

They continued on the way five days till they came to the place allotted to them. They were given ground and a wooden hut, and there they dwelt. The girl made the house pleasant for her father, and tilled the ground for vegetables. She hired herself out to labour in the fields, for all the young men were at the war. But they that worked with her looked askance at her; for she said, "Would that all were men of peace."

With winter came great cold and the snow; and the old man sickened toward death. He said, "God punish the enemy, who brought us to this." But she answered, "Alas, they are God's children and He loves them." And she said, "Rememberest thou the young man of peace?" He said, "Though the rivers pour blood into the sea, and the peoples die off like autumn leaves; though all lands be wrecked; yet shall the earth be filled full with men of peace."

He laid his hands on his daughter, blessing her; and he said, "God has need of such as thee, my daughter, my darling." Then he died, and she was alone weeping. She laid him out fairly with clean linen, and sat with the dead till dawn, thinking about death.

On a spring evening as she came home through the fields, the young man stood before her who had said, "I am a man of peace." He said, "Because of thee I became a soldier, for my heart smote me. Because of thee I put off my self-righteousness, and fought gladly. But it happened that I chased a man with steel and he tripped. And my hand would not strike him, because he had tripped. A great horror of killing came over me, so that I fled like one mad. I have done with soldiering for ever, though I die for it. That I might tell thee, I have sought thee very many days." Now the girl wondered at his words; and she began to love him. And they two wandered about among the fields, loath to part; but at last they came into her garden, and stood still among the green things. She said, "See the stars, God's children also. Surely they love, and kill not." But he told her about the stars, that they are great suns and worlds; and she said, "They that dwell in those worlds, what of them?" She lifted up her hands to heaven, greeting those peoples; and she said to them, "Brothers and sisters whom I know not; do ye work and weep and love? Then I love you. Do ye hate and kill and make war? Still I love you." Then were they two silent a while before the majesty of the stars, and the mystery of one another. He said, "I knew not what God might be, till thou didst show me. He is the majesty of all the stars, and he is the soul of one girl."

Men came seeking him who arrested him as a deserter. They said, "Brave men are dying, and thou lurkest with a harlot." The young man broke loose raging, and hurt them. But they overpowered him and killed him, and took away the body.

The girl stood still in the pathway of the garden, among the green things. She lifted up her hands again to the heavens, and to the peoples therein; and she cried to them, "Weep with me, weep with me, ye peoples. They have taken my friend." But she wept not. She stood looking from star to star, amazed at death. A great terror and joy seized her because of the near prescence of her friend.

> God sowed a seed. It shall not fail.
> Though in autumn the leaves wither.

The earth was a battlefield, and the cities heaps of ruins. All men were fighting: there were none to work. The armies were hungry and very tired, and still they fought. Women and children lay dead in the open unburied, yet more babies were born. Pestilences ate the peoples; the earth was foul.

Fiercer and fiercer grew the war, and neither side could conquer. The peoples began to rebel, and confusion grew. Yet in all lands were men of peace, working against war; and women of peace, who would not bear sons for the slaughter. Soldiers began to mingle with the enemy and be friends with them between the battles; yet at a word of command they would go back to kill. Everyone said to himself, "War is Hell; there is no good in it." But to his neighbour he said, "We suffer in a great cause." And so war devoured all things and all evil grew.

There was a woman on a battlefield, tending the wounded. The sun burned them and there was no water. They began to rave, but nothing could be done. The woman was busy over them, but all the while she thought deeply, wondering that men endured so much for war, but for peace they dared nothing.

Now a great mass of men ran thither, chased by the enemy; who slaughtered them as they ran. The woman stood up against them compassionate, but she could not restrain them. They all swept past her raging, and she was left with the newly fallen. But after a while the enemy returned bringing prisoners. They would have seized her; but a holy anger came over her, so that they dared not. She cried, "Friends, ye all hate war; why must ye fight? Are ye mad, that ye can love and yet kill? Or are ye cowards, that ye dare not throw down your weapons? The whole world wants peace, and the whole world is afraid. See the battlefield, your work! Are ye glad of it? Ye hate it, ye hate it, for ye are men, not wolves. Ye have wives and mothers and sweethearts, and children trust you. How can ye kill under the blue sky in June? Oh, we have all lost sight of God, and so we have no joy. Yet God is in everyone that loves; he is in everyone's heart. Throw down your weapons, throw them down. Better die than kill. Better die men of peace, than live making war. If ye dare, others will dare, and others and others; and so war must end."

A crowd gathered round her to listen, and each man knew that she spoke the truth; for in everyone's heart a voice answered her voice, the God in each speaking. A murmur rose from the crowd, so that all knew that all approved. And they began throwing down their weapons; and suddenly all shouted for joy. Then the women urged them to scatter over the country-side to speak for peace. And she said, "Most will be killed, but it is for peace."

Suddenly their enemy attacked them, and they let themselves be overpowered. Most were quickly destroyed, but they died praising peace. The enemy were amazed, and faltered in the killing; and soon they also threw away their weapons, and became men of peace.

All that mixed host spread abroad to persuade men to stop war. Many were martyred, but they died in joy. And the peoples were ready to hear; so the word spread. At last it was agreed that on a certain day all war should cease, and all weapons be gathered together and destroyed. And on that day it was done. Each man took a vow, holding the hand of one that had been an enemy. All the armies marched home, and in their homes was joy.

Then men began to build again what had been destroyed, and to set on foot the great works of peace. Everywhere there was sorrow still, and the misery that war had made; but there was hope. Men began to quarrel and to grasp what was within reach; but a new spirit also dawned. The souls of men had been chastened for the beginning of a new age. It shall be an age of knowing God, and an age of joy.

The woman went back to her village and made a home for herself. She grew green stuff for market, and kept fowls. She went to market every week, carrying a full basket. Her neighbours' children loved her and gave her a pet name. And often at night she went into the garden to look at the stars, and to ask them about her friend who was dead. She named the stars according to her fancy, knowing them so well. She grew to hear the music that is the song of all the stars. And she knew her friend, and he was God. Then in the time when joy had come back into the world, she died.

God sowed a seed, and there came a flower.
Holy is God, and the world His flower.

THE ROAD TO THE AIDE POST

(1916)

[This is the earliest published prose fiction by Stapledon.)]

In Belgium at two o'clock in the morning, an ambulance driver stepped out of his car and yawned. It had rained since the previous night and the world was very wet. But at last the west wind was victoriously pursuing the clouds, piling their disordered companies one upon another. Suddenly the moon shone. White ruined houses on one side of the street, huddled like sheep, looked towards the East and the star shells. Dark ruined houses on the other side held their broken walls and rafters against the sky. The driver stood for a moment watching: he began a sigh, but successfully turned it into a yawn, and moved away to prepare his car for two stretcher cases. Then he walked into the place that was once a children's playground, toward the Aide post, once the school cellar. How slow they were to-night in bringing out the school cellar. How slow they were to-night in bringing out the wounded? He examined a new hole where a shell had gone through the building. He stood by a heap of debris and watched the moon. A mighty white upright cloud was flying overhead. He looked up the sides of it as if he were standing at the foot of some extravagant aerial leaning tower of Pisa, for ever falling upon him through a sky visibly deep as the universe. The moon looked at him in that significant way of hers, as if she were desperately trying to tell him some good news. For a moment he stood fascinated by this sudden beauty. Then he remembered himself, and carefully yawned in the face of the moon.

They brought out the wounded; one moaning, the other silent; the one face half hidden under rugs and miserably moving; the other face wholly hidden under white bandages. The stretchers were soon stowed on board, driver and brancardier took their seats, and the old bus crept down the street.

The moaning man moaned with regularity, save when the car bumped him into a cry. The other lay still. What an embusqué slacker I am! thought the driver What must these old fellows think of me? The moaning man was a vieux papa for whom war was an incongruous, last chapter to a life of tilling and begetting. It was incongruous, but he had not complained. Gallantry was not his line, but he had not shirked anything that he was expected to do. Now he lay absorbed in his pain, praying for the end of the journey, or losing himself among grotesque visions of crops and beast and bursting shells, only to find himself once more in a furnace of pain. The other lay still; no one can guess where his spirit wandered, upon the earth or in the hollow sky. It's a miserable game, thought the driver, Why didn't I enlist long ago? He had no peace principles, and he disliked people, who said they were pacifists. War might be a horrible mistake, but his soldier friends in Gallipoli and Flanders were dying well. They had excelled themselves. Better make a hideous mistake and suffer with one's fellows than be a lone prig. For him, war was not scientific hate; it was love gone mad. England demanded him, and England was a nearer thing than God. Besides, who said it was wrong to fight? The best things were won by fighting; and God fought Satan. What a Paradise Lost if God had been a pacifist!

So thought the driver, as he drove down moonlit avenues. At the hospital, the car was unloaded, and he saw the two broken men carried through the door that had received so many like them.

Now in the early dawn that driver came hurrying back. There was a rose pink glow in the East, as if no ill had ever come out of that quarter; as if hate were never in this world. Into this fairy land he drove, and the joy of morning began in him. But the gentle appearance of things did not shake his resolution. Surely, surely, he must enlist, and give his life with his friends. The Red Cross was not a heavy enough cross for such as he. The sunrise swallowed aid that was left of the night; the whole sky was on fire. He would go, he would go. What was he that he should judge, when so many finer men had not hesitated to fight? His Quaker parents would be very grieved, but he must do it. He himself was unhappy thinking of his parents' grief. After all war was indeed a hideous thing. In fact his determination to fight began already his disillusionment. A secret voice saying You will fight only because you are ashamed not to fight. You will fight for you own peace of mind, not for victory, not for the cause. You have not forgotten yourself in the cause. You will not even find the peace of mind you seek. The sun flashed from behind the Eastern cloudbank and the trees and fields and sparkling canal seemed suddenly to laugh, so bright they grew. Oh God, what a world! cried the driver aloud while the car roared along. The sun and the countryside undoubtedly confirmed that secret voice now that he allowed himself to attend to them.

He had heard someone say that just as private killing went out of date so will war someday go also, and that this War is but the red dawn of a new age wherein many obscurities will be enlightened. Surely if Peace and Goodwill could not be the idea of to-day they would be the idea of to-morrow. Woe unto those who, having any inkling of that great idea of to-morrow, desert it even for the highest of to-day's ideals. The Fates had made him to have some glimpse of the dawn, before his fighting friends: Woe to him if he closed his eyes.

Not happy, nor content, nor even positive, was he on his return; but very sure that he would not fight. His vision of the new idea (which is also so old an idea) was very faint; but it was a vision, and commanded his allegiance. Perhaps after all he was making a mistake; but it was a noble mistake. The vision must be followed even at the risk of his soul's life.

The driver backed his car into its place; stumped into the camp, pulled his best enemy out of bed, persuaded the puppy to lick the cook's slumbering face; and began his morning toilet. Many times again he was tempted in that wilderness of doubt. Each time the vision was a little clearer than before.

He is a type, is he not?

Lector House believes that a society develops through a two-fold approach of continuous learning and adaptation, which is derived from the study of classic literary works spread across the historic timeline of literature records. Therefore, we aim at reviving, repairing and redeveloping all those inaccessible or damaged but historically as well as culturally important literature across subjects so that the future generations may have an opportunity to study and learn from past works to embark upon a journey of creating a better future.

This book is a result of an effort made by Lector House towards making a contribution to the preservation and repair of original ancient works which might hold historical significance to the approach of continuous learning across subjects.

HAPPY READING & LEARNING!

LECTOR HOUSE LLP
E-MAIL: lectorpublishing@gmail.com